The
Griffin
Legacy

YEARLING BOOKS are designed especially to entertain and enlighten young people. Charles F. Reasoner, Professor Emeritus of Children's Literature and Reading, New York University, is consultant to this series.

For a complete listing of all Yearling titles,
write to Dell Publishing Co., Inc.,
Promotion Department, P.O. Box 3000,
Pine Brook, N.J. 07058.

THE GRIFFIN LEGACY

Jan O'Donnell Klaveness

A YEARLING BOOK

Published by
Dell Publishing Co., Inc.
1 Dag Hammarskjold Plaza
New York, New York 10017

Yearling ® TM 913705, Dell Publishing Co., Inc.

ISBN: 0-440-43165-4

Reprinted by arrangement with Macmillan Publishing
Company, a division of Macmillan, Inc.

Printed in the United States of America

First Yearling printing—December 1985

CW

IN MEMORY OF CHARLES ROBERT O'DONNELL

AND FOR MY FAMILY,

WITH LOVE AND APPRECIATION OF

OUR OWN LEGACY

Contents

I

The House on Constitution Hill

Slowly the crest of Constitution Hill unfolded beneath the early morning mists, revealing first the black trunk of a huge elm, then a gray sweep of lawn, and finally the blurred outline of the white shingled house, exactly as it was in the photograph. But that yellowed image, framed and hung in her father's study for as long as Amy Enfield could remember, had not prepared her for the reality of the house itself. Hunched on the shoulder of the hill, it was weather-beaten and uninviting, a dispiriting presence in the landscape.

The taxi driver shifted into low for the last steep grade up Bridge Street, and swung right onto the pitted gravel driveway. Amy gripped the handle of her suitcase tightly as the cab stopped next to the back door. Up close the shingles of the house were a scarred, graying white; the screen on the door was poorly patched, and the door itself had worn a groove where it scraped on the slanted back porch. Amy clung to her suitcase, waiting, but the house remained still and lifeless, its sagging disrepair offering no welcome.

"You're sure they're expecting you, young lady?" The taxi driver turned around to her, his arm over the front seat. "It's mighty early, even for farm folk."

Amy sat motionless on the cracked leather seat, staring at the closed house. "My father wrote. I mailed the letter myself."

The driver switched off the ignition. "All right, then. You go give a knock while I get your bags."

He came around to open her door and went on to unlock the trunk of the car. Damp, cool air swirled into the cab and still Amy sat, hesitant to step out, afraid to become part of this unknown yet oddly familiar landscape. It seemed incredible that she was here at all, that her parents had sent her even temporarily to live in the old homestead on Constitution Hill. Yet here she was, as misplaced and confused as if they had whisked her by magic into the faded photograph on the study wall. And she couldn't go back; there was nothing to go back to. While 1946 had brought an end to world-wide upheaval, had returned most families to normal routines of birth and marriage and death, it had shaken and upended Amy's world. Her father's government work ended with the war, and his new company was located in the Midwest. Their house, the only home Amy had ever known, was sold the day it went on the market. But finding a new home was not so easy. In the post-war glut of returning servicemen, housing was scarce. There were simply no affordable homes available within commuting distance of Chicago. Finally, as the school year approached, Amy's parents rented a small apartment for themselves and arranged to send Amy to stay with her grandmother.

"You'll love the country," her father said as they waited for her train in the Baltimore station. "There are all kinds of hills and trees to climb, lots of open space. Things aren't all pushed together the way they are in the city."

"And Grandma, you'll love being with Grandma," her mother added, a catch in her voice. "She'll spoil you completely."

"Not if Aunt Matilda can help it," Mr. Enfield said, smiling. "Watch out for her."

Then they hugged her and put her on the train north, and an hour later they boarded a train west, spinning out and away from home like fragments from a dying star. No, Amy couldn't go back, and she couldn't remain indefinitely in the taxi. She stepped out onto the mist-slick gravel and slammed the car door.

The shade in the kitchen window overlooking the drive snapped up, flapping noisily around its roller. A moment later the window slammed up, and as suddenly slammed down again. Amy looked at the taxi driver. He set the two large suitcases down in the driveway, looked back at her, and shrugged.

"At least we know there's someone home," he said.

Tightening her grip on her overnight bag, Amy stepped up onto the slanted porch and lifted her hand to knock. Her fingers had not touched the wood when the inside door was flung open. A round, lined face peered out through the gray screening.

"Grandma? It's Amy. I'm here."

"Amy!" The screen door scraped back as a woman not much taller than Amy, with sandy white hair, shoved it impatiently open and stepped out. "Amy, just look at you! I'd never have recognized you. You've grown up!"

"Yes, ma'am. I guess so."

"And while you grew up, I grew down . . . and out," she added, patting her broad hips. She smiled then, let the screen door scrape to behind her, and opened her arms to Amy. "But you aren't too old to hug."

Her plump hands were warm and firm around Amy's shoulders, and the soft wrinkled cheek that pressed against Amy's smooth one smelled of Noxzema and carnations mixed with the yeasty odor of rising bread. The years shrank away, and Amy saw herself a toddler on the red brick patterned kitchen floor in the house in Maryland, a piece of rapidly graying yeast dough in her hands, with Grandma punching down the white, fluffy mass in the brown crockery bowl, making kuchen for Christmas morning. That was Grandma's last visit before Aunt Matilda's health failed, before the war, before the long period of gas rationing and conservation of tires that restricted traveling and divided families.

"You're here. You're really here!" Grandma exclaimed, pulling back to look at Amy at arm's length. Her eyes were wet and sparkling, and her smile wavered. "It's been so long. Who would have thought? Can it really be eight years?"

"I'm almost fourteen, Grandma."

"Fourteen, is it? Of course, almost fourteen indeed." She hugged Amy once again. The taxi driver cleared his throat.

"Have you paid the man, child?" Grandma dabbed at her eyes with her apron, blinking rapidly at Amy. "Put the bags there in the kitchen. No need to be standing out here all morning long."

When the driver had been paid and dismissed, Grandma shepherded Amy into the kitchen. The room was warm and fragrant with the smell of fresh coffee and doughnuts, reminding Amy of how hungry she was. While Grandma read the letter Amy's father had sent with her, Amy sat down and ate doughnuts and drank a mug of hot milk flavored with coffee. When her appetite was somewhat satisfied, she looked around curiously. She had seen the old house only in her father's photograph, only from the outside. Now she examined the long-imagined interior. The kitchen, a large, square room, had a pantry in one corner for the canned tomatoes and fruits Grandma put up each summer. It was clean, but cluttered, with stacks of newspapers beside the refrigerator, and clippings pinned on the cupboard and calendar. Most of all it was old, and in spite of the modern sink, refrigerator, and stove, it was dominated by the huge open hearth where three generations of Griffins had cooked.

Grandma looked old, too, or maybe just old-fashioned. Amy was accustomed to people her parents' age, tall, straight men, and women who curled their hair and wore make-up and stylish clothes. Neither tall nor stylish, Grandma was thick, solid from shoulders to knees, and rather shapeless beneath the layers of sweaters and aprons. Her sandy white hair was pulled back in a bun from which strands loosened and fell around her face. She poked them back absently as she read.

"It seems you're to be here for a while," she said at last, folding the letter and tucking it into her apron pocket. As though she could read Amy's mind, she added, "Which suits me just fine. But it has been a long time since there was a youngster in this house. It will take some getting used to, for all of us. I'm not as young as I used to be, and Auntie. . . ."

Above their heads a steady thumping began. Grandma frowned. "There she is now, wanting her breakfast. She knew you were coming, but she may have forgotten. I'll just remind her that you're here, and tell her again who you are and all. She gets a little confused sometimes. And you'll have to speak up. She's hard of hearing. Here, you take the tray and I'll bring the teapot."

Amy took the tray and followed her grandmother from the kitchen through the dining room and up the wide, banistered stairway. The sun was fully up now and the mists had burned away, but the house was dim, shadowed by the great elm in the yard. At the top of the stairs her grandmother turned right, opened a dark oak door, and led Amy into a high-ceilinged, heavily curtained room. In its center was a canopied fourposter covered with a patchwork quilt. Until Grandma pulled back the drapes, Amy thought the bed was empty. As her eyes adjusted to the change in the light, she made out the form of a tiny woman, the quilt pulled up to her chin. The figure lay quite still, staring straight up at the white canopy, her face as pale as the pillow cover, blue veins showing clearly in the hollows of her temples. Only her hand moved, thumping a gold-headed cane slowly, regularly, on the wide oak floor.

"It's about time you got here, Louise," she said in a low, surprisingly strong voice. The cane stopped thumping. Pushing down on it, the old woman raised herself slowly, still looking straight ahead. The bones of her face stood out, chiseled by age beneath the tissue-thin skin, her nose a sharp aquiline bridge between high, flat cheekbones.

"Amy's here, Matilda. Remember, Paul's daughter? I told you she was coming."

"Of course I remember. Get my glasses, Louise. I can't see her without my glasses."

Amy remained in the center of the room with the breakfast tray, trying not to stare. She knew, of course, that her great-aunt, Grandma's half sister, lived in the old house, that she had lived there all her life. Aunt Matilda and her husband, Uncle Plyn, had farmed the land and had helped Grandma to raise Paul, Amy's father. In the family album there were yellowed photographs of Auntie, dressed always in long black skirts with white aprons. But those yellowed features bore no resemblance to the tiny, skeletal creature propped up on pillows in the great bed. Amy's gaze slipped again and again from Auntie's face to the gnarled, mottled hand holding her cane, both fascinated and repelled by the fragile yet tenacious grip.

"So you're young Paul's daughter. Come here, child, and let me get a look at you." Auntie slipped on her glasses and turned her head toward Amy. Behind the thick lenses her eyes were a milky blue, as though they reflected past memories from within her head more easily than they looked out on the present. "Come here, I say. Put down that tray and come here."

Amy hesitated, then approached the bed.

"Sit down, here." The cane thumped the edge of the mattress. Amy set her tray down on the bedside table and perched beside her great-aunt. She sat very still as the old lady inspected her, forcing herself to look back into the blank glint of the glasses. Slowly the old woman drew her hand from under the covers and stretched it out toward Amy's face. The knuckles were thickened with arthritis, making the tiny hand tight and crimped like a claw. Instinctively Amy pulled back.

"There's nothing to be afraid of, child. I need my hands to help me see." The bony, blue-veined hand reached out and touched Amy's face, feeling first the cheek, then sliding up across her eyes to her forehead, and down again over her nose to her mouth. Her hand was cold and dry, scuttling lightly over the surface of Amy's face, recording in detail what Aunt Matilda's eyes no longer could. "You're an Enfield, all right. You've got your grandfather's eyes, just like Paul. Doesn't she, Louise? But your bones are Griffin bones, like mine and your grandmother's. You're a Griffin, make no mistake."

"My name is Enfield, Amy Enfield," Amy said, as much to reassure herself as to remind the old woman of her identity.

"Names aren't important. It's blood and bones that count." She nodded, still inspecting Amy through the thick glasses. "You'll do. To think that your father never sent you here to see us until now, when Plyn's gone and I can barely see the tip of my own nose."

"It wasn't his fault, Matilda." Grandma poured the tea and set it on the tray. "We all had to wait until the war ended."

"That's all this family ever does, is wait for some war or other to end. For us it was the First World War, and for my father it was the Civil War. And before that there was the

Revolutionary War, when it all started." She closed her eyes as if to shut out the present, to see more clearly into the faded past. But in a moment she was awake, her gaze fixed once more on Amy. Leaning back on her pillows, she laid the gold-headed cane beside her on the bed. "It's an heirloom," she said, as though in answer to a question. "Belonged to my great-grandfather, and to his father before that. You know about the family?"

Amy shook her head. "Not very much."

"Your father never told you?"

"I guess I never asked."

"That's the trouble with people today. They don't take the time to learn history. Do you make friends easily?"

"I don't know. I guess so."

"Good. That will make it easier, much easier. But you must be receptive, open, even to things you don't understand. That's how you make friends, slowly. All right, child. Get up now and let me have my breakfast." Her blue opaque eyes held Amy's for a moment, then she lifted the napkin on the tray and looked at her breakfast. "Cereal again, Louise?"

"You know what the doctor said."

"I was there, wasn't I? But I think I'd prefer dying to living on this diet. We're all too long-lived in this family anyway. Why, my grandmother, with the hard life she had, lived well into her seventies, and my father was in his eighties when he died. At the rate I'm going, I'll outdo them both. Have you explored the house yet, child?"

"No, ma'am. I just got here."

"Then don't be sitting there gawking at me while I eat. You've got a lot of looking to do. You can unpack later. Go on now."

As Amy closed the bedroom door, she heard her great-aunt's low voice. "You did put her in the old wing, Louise? In my old room, didn't you?"

"Since you insisted, Matilda, though I can't believe that it matters."

"The legacy matters," Auntie said as the door clicked shut, muffling the rest of her words. Amy stood in the long, dim hall and listened, hearing only the muted clank of silver on china as Aunt Matilda ate her breakfast. Heavy oak doors loomed on either side of her, closed upon the past. She shivered. One of those doors opened onto the room she was to have, the room once occupied by Aunt Matilda, whose blinded eyes looked back in time so keenly.

Amy started away from Aunt Matilda's door, pulling her hand from the knob as if it were a red-hot poker. This was a strange old house her parents had abandoned her to, and Auntie was a strange and forbidding old lady.

"I'll stay away from her until they send for me," she decided. "After all, it's just until Mom and Dad get settled."

But suppose it took them months, a year, to settle? Rattling and banging all night on the train up the East Coast, Amy had had no time to be homesick. Now the memory of home burst upon her with peppermint sharpness, of her parents at breakfast that last morning, the smell of coffee and chrysanthemums picked from the garden. Her throat ached and tears pricked her eyes. Banished from that warm, sunny present to this dim old house, she would have given all its legacies to turn the clock back a mere twenty-four hours.

"But I am here," she whispered to the dark oaken doors. "I'm here, and I've got to stay here. So I might as well find out just where I am." She glanced once more at the closed door of Auntie's room, then turned and started down the stairs.

At the foot of the staircase was a wide, slate-floored hall

into which the front door opened from the porch outside. To the right was the dining room with a doorway into the kitchen. White wainscoting ran halfway up the walls, with a yellowing, patterned paper above it. The side windows looked out on the driveway, and the two at the front of the house opened onto the veranda. The furniture was simple, rather old she supposed, consisting of a trestle table and captain's chairs, a large pine hutch, and a dry sink filled with tuberous begonias. Amy turned to the left, to the living room.

It, too, had windows overlooking the porch and the front yard, shaded by the elm. The windows at the rear of the room looked into the backyard. But where there were side windows in the dining room, here there was a huge fireplace with an oak mantel, and a solid piece of oak paneling set above it from mantel to ceiling. Hanging against the dark wood was a portrait. Intending to go out on the porch, Amy merely glanced at it. But the painted blue eyes caught her own and looked directly at her. Amy stepped into the room. The eyes of the painting held hers. She moved to one side, toward the front of the house. The eyes seemed to follow. Amy turned to the center of the room. Again the eyes followed her and continued to stare at her as she walked to the back windows. When she sat down in the rocker by the fireplace, the portrait still watched. Amy got up and stared into the face above her.

It was the portrait of a young woman, seated sedately with her hands crossed on a Book of Common Prayer. In spite of the pose, she seemed about to laugh. The morning sun shone through the elm branches, touching the painting in flickers of light and shadow. Amy smiled at the face. For all its stiffness, this was the portrait of a girl who liked fun, someone Amy would like to have known. She could imagine the painted braids coming undone with running, the long skirts hiked up to swing from birch trees or to walk fence rails. Staring at the eyes, Amy could have sworn the lips of the painting smiled back. And when she looked at the mouth, it seemed the eyes twinkled. Amy was still concentrating on the face, trying to catch its least movement, when she heard her grandmother behind her on the stairs.

"Amy? There you are." She carried the tray with her into the living room. "So you've already found the other resident of the house. She wasn't much older than you when that was painted. She's been on the wall there as long as I can remember."

"Did she ever smile at you?"

"At me? No, she never smiled at me." Grandma looked up at the portrait and chuckled. "But you aren't the first to ask, or the first to notice her expression. It's only the light through the elm tree that makes her smile, I've always thought. Lord knows, she did little enough laughing while she lived. Come along now. You can help me do up these dishes and we'll get you settled in your room."

"Yes, ma'am." Amy hesitated, glancing again at the girl in the painting, but the face had lapsed into flatness beneath the dappling sunlight.

II

Auntie's Room

"This part of the house has been closed for years," Grandma said, turning left at the top of the stairs. "Since your Aunt Matilda married and moved into the wing with Uncle Plyn. But it's big and sunny, this room is, and we thought you'd like it."

"It was Auntie's room?"

"When she was a girl. That was before I was born. You see, my father was a widower. Auntie is his first wife's daughter. He was nearly fifty when he married my mother and started a whole second family. Here we are." She set down Amy's suitcase and opened one of the oak doors. The room was on the front of the house, above the dining room. White priscilla curtains fluttered at the windows, there was a braided rag rug on the floor, and a neatly made spindle bed with crocheted spread. The whole room smelled of clean, sun-dried sheets and camphor.

"Now, while you unpack, I'll help Auntie go downstairs. Just put your things in the chest of drawers there and hang what you can in the clothes press. Whatever doesn't fit, you'll have to put in the clothes press in the hall."

"Clothes press?"

"That's New England for closet," Grandma said, laughing. "Probably because the closets are so small they press the clothes together! I'll be back to help you after I get Auntie settled."

"Grandma? Grandma, wait." Amy stopped her as she stepped out into the hallway and was closing the heavy oak door behind her. "Why did you give me this room?"

"I told you, child," Grandma answered, turning back in surprise. "We thought you'd like it, being in the old wing and all."

"You and Aunt Matilda? But suppose I don't."

"Let's worry about that when the time comes." Grandma smiled, her face softening in a series of plump wrinkles, and slipped her arm around Amy's shoulders. "It's all very strange now, but before you know it, you'll feel right at home."

"And if I don't, may I move closer to you? Aunt Matilda won't mind?"

"Of course not." Grandma gave her a reassuring squeeze. "Don't you worry about Auntie. She's spent a lot of years on this earth, and she has some pretty firm ideas about life, past and present. Sometimes she's a bit peculiar, that's all, a little odd. But we're all going to get along just fine. Now, you get on with your business, and I'll get on with mine. If you need me, I'm just down the hall."

Left alone, Amy remained standing in the doorway, looking into the room. It was pleasant enough, and sunny as Grandma had said. The windows were generously proportioned so that the morning light reached into its farthest corners. And there was a harmony in the very dimensions of the room that was complemented by the simple, unadorned furniture. In spite of herself, Amy responded to its open, airy charm. Her reservations about occupying Auntie's room receded, and she entered, crossing to look out the front window.

Bridge Street dropped down the hill in narrow gray strips

between a border of oaks and maples to meet with the main road that bisected the valley. On the far side of the valley Amy could see the rolling line of the Berkshire Hills, and far off to the left, the peak of Mt. Greylock. Directly below her window was the green front lawn, blending with the open meadow that stretched down to the highway. Rooftops poked through the yellowing September foliage, and one church steeple was visible to the left of the meadow, near the road.

The view was oddly familiar, like a model railway layout Amy might have seen in a department store during the holidays. The tiny houses on the far hillside looked too neat and trim to be real. Next to the gleaming white church spire they seemed insubstantial, dispensable squares on the total pattern of the valley. Amy stared at the church, trying to make the rest of it out through the thick clumps of trees. But in addition to the huge elm in the front yard, there was another giant tree just behind the church at the bottom of the hill, and the two effectively screened the building. Still she remained at the window, looking down into the valley. Leaning there in the warm morning sunshine, her hand touching the aged, grooved sill, Amy felt the peace and quiet of the old house well up around her, absorbing the shock of the rapid changes that had brought her here. She took a deep breath and wriggled her shoulders, releasing the tension in her neck. At last everything seemed to be slowing down, giving her a chance to catch up with herself. Some tightness inside her began to uncoil, as though feathery fingers were gently clicking into place the secret combination to her inner locked self. She yawned and stretched, suddenly overwhelmed by a desire to sleep. Through half-closed eyes she saw the details of the scene below her fade and blur, the huge trees wavering and shrinking in size. There was a rushing in her ears, not of sound, but of utter silence, a deafening stillness. Amy blinked rapidly and shook her head. She sat down abruptly on the bed, dizzy and off-balance.

"That's what riding all night on a train will do to you," she said to herself. "Even after you get off, you keep jouncing. I guess I'm more tired than I thought." She stood up carefully, holding onto the carved post of the bedstead. The cherry wood was turned out in a series of graceful designs, ending in an acornlike knob at the top. The feel of the wood on her palm was comforting. She was still standing there when she heard Grandma and Auntie in the hallway.

"Let me just see how she's doing, Louise. We want to be sure that our guest is comfortable."

The footsteps came slowly down the hall and stopped at Amy's room. There was a tap on the door, and Grandma peeked in.

"Why, you haven't even begun to unpack yet." She stood in the doorway with Auntie leaning half on her arm, half on the gold-headed cane. "You'll still be working at lunchtime."

"Leave her alone, Louise. She's just getting acquainted, aren't you, child? It's a good room, a room with many memories. Take your time getting to know it. Make friends slowly."

They turned away from the doorway, and Amy heard them on the stairs, the slow footsteps punctuated by the thump of the cane.

By noon Amy had finished not only her unpacking, but her inspection of the room. If there were any unexpected friends to be found, she preferred to come upon them in broad daylight, not in the moonlit dark of midnight. Aside from the bed, which was squeaky but comfortable, there were a bureau and table in the room. Both were unremarkable, solid and practical. The only thing of interest was a Bible on the nightstand at the head of the bed. It was an old, leatherbound volume, cracking at the binding. When Amy opened it, brown crumbs of paper spilled into her lap. Inside, the flyleaf was covered with spindly writing, brown and faded at the top, darkening toward the bottom. The last entry was her own name and birthdate, beneath those of her parents, in neatly printed black letters. A connecting line went up from her father's name to her grandmother's, with Grandpa Paul's full name and years of his birth and death written next to hers.

"Paul Robert Enfield," Amy read. "Born 1880, died 1910."

Such a short life he had had. It was odd to see his full name written out, as though they had finally been introduced, grandfather and granddaughter. He was a stranger to her, a stranger even to his own son, who had been only two years old when his father died. Amy followed along the dark line to the entries above it. The ink lightened in color as it went back to the earlier generations of the family. Below the first faint names were those of their children and their children's children, widening down the page like a lily pad growing from the surface of time into a tangled future of roots and stems.

There was Aunt Matilda, daughter of Amy's great-grandfather and his first wife. Auntie was born in 1861, which made her now, Amy figured carefully, eighty-five years old. That she had been alive during the Civil War made her ancient in Amy's eyes, a relic of another era. Skipping to the top of the page, Amy deciphered the name of Philo Coburn, married to a barely visible Martha. Their four children were listed on the line below—Thomas, Lucy, Edward, and Anne. The script was ornate, and Amy puzzled over the faint curlicues and flourishes. Of the four children, only Lucy had lived to marry and bear children of her own. Thomas and Edward, from the dates of their deaths, must have fought and died in the Revolutionary War. And Anne, Amy noted with a pang in spite of the century that separated them, had died of some unnamed ailment at the age of fourteen.

"Amy?" Her grandmother was calling from the bottom of the stairs. "Amy, lunch is ready. Can you come down?"

"Yes, ma'am." With some relief, Amy closed the book. But instead of replacing it on the nightstand, she carried it downstairs with her. "I found this in my room," she began, setting it down on the kitchen table.

"Why, how ever did it get there? It belongs in the parlor, on the stand."

"I put it there, Louise." Auntie was already seated at the table. "The child has to learn about her family somehow."

Amy glanced nervously at the old woman. "The writing's awfully faint. I could hardly make it out."

"I don't need to see it, child. It's all here." She tapped her head with a bony finger. "Every birth and death from Philo Coburn down to your generation. If I'd been a boy, I'd have been named after him."

"Philo Coburn?"

"The same. An Englishman by birth, a patriot by persuasion, he built this house and raised his family here. He was a proud and stubborn man."

"And Amy's a famished fourteen-year-old. Put the book away now," Grandma said, "and let's have lunch."

Amy removed the book and helped her grandmother set out soup and sandwiches. While they ate, Grandma talked about the Fair, the annual celebration of the town's colonial heritage.

"We'll go down to the church tomorrow," she said. "You'll have to help me pack up the preserves this afternoon. And we'll have to find you a costume. There ought to be something up in the trunk to fit you."

"I have to dress up?"

"Everyone does, Amy. It's like going back in time two hundred years. You'll enjoy it. And you'll get a chance to meet some of the village young people."

"Don't you let her get mixed up with those Winters children, Louise. We don't want them poking around here."

Grandma shook her head and sighed. "Now, Matilda, you mustn't take on so. We'll be driving to church with the Winterses. They're fine youngsters, Ben and Betsy."

The light flashed off Auntie's glasses as she looked over at Grandma, but she only nodded to herself. "Take some of the mums along, Louise. We can plant them in the family plot. The dahlias will be finished by now."

"Just as soon as I get the preserves ready, Matilda." Grandma began to clear the table. "You've seen the rest of the house, Amy. You might as well find out where the root cellar is."

At the back of the house was a sloping, hatch door. Grandma lifted the latch and swung back the wooden cover. Stone steps led down into the darkness, which gave off the scent of cool, sunless earth. Grandma reached up and found the light, a single socket hanging from the ceiling. It was a small room, with walls formed by round chunks of New England rock. There were wooden shelves on three sides, stacked with jars of preserves and home-canned vegetables. On the fourth side was a table, bins of potatoes and carrots beneath it. Grandma set down her trays and looked around.

"Let's see now. Which shall we take this year? The strawberry always goes well. It's the rector's favorite. That shelf there on your right, Amy, has the pint jars. Take a dozen of those, and of the currant jelly right next to it." She took a cloth from the table and dusted off the jars as Amy handed them to her. "When Plyn was alive we had so much more. He used to tap maples for sugar and syrup. Everyone wanted some of

Plyn's maple syrup. Now it's all I can do to keep up with the berries."

Amy set the last three jars of jelly on the table and looked at the objects arranged along the back of the table. "What's that?"

Grandma laughed and pulled one of the things over. It was a wooden tub with a flat plate on top, connected to a screw handle. "That's a small wine press. The grapes we didn't use for jam or jelly Plyn would use to make wine. In the old days they had a small vineyard here, with vines Philo Coburn's wife brought from Germany. Good wine it was, too, Matilda says. There was an old carved wooden cask to age it in and a celebration every fall when the new wine came in."

Amy looked around. "Is it still here?"

"I doubt it, dear. Though I remember sneaking down here with my brother Johnny to play at Robin Hood, or at being locked in a dungeon like the Count of Monte Cristo. It was still here then, along with the old tin cup and saucer Plyn used for tasting the wine. And how we'd torment him!" She laughed again. "I shouldn't tell you the tricks we played on old Plyn, surprising him down here reading the paper when Matilda was after him to slop the hogs or take the honey wagon over the fields. Many's the penny candy we got not to tell her where he was. Of course, she always knew anyway. I'd swear that woman had eyes in the back of her head. But listen to me ramble on. My stars, Amy, it makes me young again just to have you in the house."

She set her dusting cloth down and turned her back on the table. Hands on hips, Grandma surveyed the root cellar. "I don't suppose it would hurt to look around a little. Let's see. Johnny and I used that corner for the dungeon, and over there was where the jailer sat, right next to the wine barrel."

In a moment Grandma was pulling crocks and mason jars

from the corners of the cellar, swiping at cobwebs and sneezing in the dust she raised. On her hands and knees, Amy crawled into the far jailer's corner. There, tilted against the wall, was all that was left of the wine barrel.

"Grandma, it's beautiful!" Amy rubbed away the sticky webs on the face of the barrel and ran her fingers over the carved surface. Grape leaves and bunches of grapes bordered the round keg head, and just above the spigot that the wine had flowed through was the date 1770. "We ought to polish it and hang it somewhere. And look, here's the tin cup and plate."

She handed the dented, blackened things to Grandma, who smiled as she rubbed them on her apron. "Certainly does bring back memories. Dear Johnny, and Plyn, both dead now. Matilda is the only one who really remembers that time." She sighed and returned the cup and saucer to Amy. "But memories aren't getting these preserves to the Fair! We'd better get back to work, my dear, before Matilda comes looking for me the way she did when I was your age."

When the trays were loaded, Grandma and Amy carried them upstairs to pack in cardboard boxes for the trip to the Fair. The polished jars of strawberry and currant, blueberry and grape, gleamed in the sun like rubies and sapphires, and the apple butter glowed softly amber, treasures wrested from the dark recesses of the earth. Grandma fussed over them, checking the labels and holding the currant jelly to the light to assure herself of its clarity. The kitchen was bright with afternoon sun, and the air crisp with the spicy scent of chrysanthemums outside the door. Temporarily forgetting Auntie, and her own homesickness, Amy whistled through her teeth as she packed the jars.

III

St. George's Church

Amy awoke slowly the next morning, prolonging the moments of half-sleep to avoid full consciousness of her new surroundings. She lay with her eyes closed, willing the mattress and pillow to feel like her own bed in Maryland, but it was no use. She opened her eyes and listened to the early morning silence of the old house. It was another clear day. From the window she could see the tops of the trees beginning to yellow into colors of fall. Amy imagined the valley in late October, filled with the russets and golds of oak and maple.

"It's beautiful in the spring as well, when the willows first yellow by the river banks, and the birches send out their green caterpillar buds."

In a voice as soft as winter snow falling, the words drifted into Amy's consciousness. Though audible, they seemed to come to her across a long distance, like echoes from a remote valley. The voice itself was young and friendly but subdued, its lilt suppressed by sadness. And then, as suddenly as it had come, it was gone—not faded away, but completely absent, replaced by the small morning noises of the birds and creatures in the meadow below.

Amy sat up and swung around on the bed to face the doorway, so sure was she that a voice had spoken the words aloud. But her room was empty, and the house remained still. Bare-footed, she crossed the room and opened the door to the hall. Auntie's door was still closed, and no sound came from her grandmother's room or from the kitchen. Nothing in the house had changed, yet the words had rung out so clearly, she could have sworn that someone else was with her by the window. Had she only been talking to herself out loud? Perhaps the voice had come from the porch just below her window. Glancing again at Auntie's door, she tiptoed down the hall to the stairs, ran down, and opened the front door. Birds sang in the elm in the yard, and dew sparkled on the lush green lawn. But there was no one in sight. As she turned away from the door, Amy's eyes caught those of the portrait in the living room as they had the day before. The face was in shadow, not yet touched by the light of the sun.

"You're up early, child."

Amy jumped at the sound of the low voice, convinced for an irrational instant that the portrait had spoken. But it was Auntie, seated in the rocker in front of the fireplace.

"Did I startle you?"

"I thought everyone was asleep." Amy hesitated, uncomfortable alone with the old woman. "Did you come downstairs by yourself? Or is Grandma awake?"

"On good days I can manage by myself. It's clear and dry today, so my arthritis isn't so bad. I like to sit here with Lucy in the mornings."

"Lucy?" Amy looked quickly around, then followed her great-aunt's nearly sightless gaze as it turned to the painting. A chill went up Amy's neck as the young painted eyes met the veiled old ones.

"Were you talking to her?" Amy asked.

The old woman looked back at Amy, then began to rock slowly. "You heard voices?"

"Not exactly. I thought someone spoke to me."

Auntie nodded and continued to rock. "My grandfather brought this rocker from Springfield for her. She'd sit on the porch and look out over the corn to the church. And in winter she'd sit here by the fire. He'd never sit in it after she died, just stand and stare at it. I remember..." Auntie's voice faded, and her eyes shifted to the empty, cold hearth. "I remember...."

Decades spun away in Amy's mind like leaves on a calendar, backward in time. Auntie seemed so incredibly old that to think beyond her, to her grandfather and great-grandmother, was as difficult as imagining infinity.

"He heard her too," the old woman muttered. "My father said it was the wind he heard, nothing but the wind in the chimney. But Charles Griffin knew better. He'd lean with his pipe on the mantelpiece, staring at the rocker as though he could still see her there."

"Charles Griffin? Who was he?"

"The Bible, child, didn't you read the Bible?" Auntie's voice was suddenly strong and direct. "Charles Griffin was my grandfather. He had two sons and a daughter. The younger son was my father and your grandmother's father."

Somewhat bewildered, Amy tried to visualize the flyleaf of the family Bible. "But I thought Philo Coburn built this house. Where did the Griffins come from?"

"So you do remember some of it." Auntie seemed pleased. She leaned back in the rocker, folded her hands, and began to recall the family history for Amy.

"Philo Coburn settled this land, all right. He settled the land and sent his two sons off to die for it. That left him with a farm and two daughters, not much help at harvest time. And right next door, on the land adjoining his, was the widower Charles Griffin. He needed a woman in his house to cook for his three sons and himself. The marriage must have seemed a logical solution to everyone's problems. Philo Coburn got a son-in-law and some manpower, Griffin got a wife."

Auntie paused, as though turning a page in her memory, then went on.

"It was a marriage of convenience. But Lucy kept her half of the bargain. Married off to that old man, she was faithful. She nursed him when he got sick, and when he died she saw him properly laid to rest. But before he was cold in the grave his sons had turned her out, sent her home to her father. Humiliated her, they did, and her the daughter of a patriot. Still, some would say she had the last word. She bore Charles Griffin's son and kept Charles Griffin's name."

"And her son, that was your grandfather."

Auntie nodded. The rocker creaked on the wide floor-boards. Amy looked from Auntie to the portrait to the mantel where Charles Griffin had rested his pipe and listened to his mother's voice.

"Could he really hear her?"

"A house this old is full of voices for those who have the ears to hear them." She fixed her pale blue gaze on Amy. "You know that."

But Amy did not want to know that. Even in the bright light of Sunday morning, Auntie's presence was a chill shadow of times gone by. The thought of being in the shade of those memories frightened Amy, and she stepped back toward the sunny hallway, shivering. Auntie was watching her, though Amy stood at the limits of her physical sight.

"You'll catch your death standing there in your bare feet and a nightdress," she said, slipping her glasses out of a pocket and onto her nose. "You'd best get your clothes on and help

Grandma with breakfast or we'll never get to church on time. Go on, child."

Amy needed no urging. She darted out of the room and up the stairs into her grandmother's room.

"Good morning, dear," Grandma said around a mouthful of hairpins. "Did you sleep well?"

"Fine, thank you." Amy watched her anchor the smooth coil of hair at the nape of her neck, steadied by her grandmother's solidly normal appearance. She had even powdered her face this morning and wore a pink touch of lipstick. Without her apron and sweaters she had a rounded but attractive figure. All in all, she looked ten years younger. "You look nice, Grandma."

"It's the old-time clothes. They suit me." She stood up and shook out the long skirt. "Reminds me of when I was a girl with button shoes and petticoats. There are some things on your bed that ought to fit you. If you need help, just call."

Spread out on Amy's bed was a challis dress of paisley print in shades of cream and rose. At the neck and sleeves it was trimmed with cream-colored lace. Beside it was a petticoat frothy with ruffles. Amy slipped out of her nightgown and layered herself into the clothes. The only mirror in the room was streaked and rippled with age. Crouching, Amy tried to get a full-length view of herself, but her reflection wobbled, stretching and shrinking like a fun house mirror image. She twirled around, looking over her shoulder. For an instant the mirror seemed to return a double image, as though her own face and another gazed from the glass. Startled, Amy stopped in mid-twirl and stood still. As her swinging skirts wrapped around her legs, then settled slowly in folds around her ankles, she looked carefully around the empty room. The face she had seen, like so many other things in the old house, was vaguely familiar yet not recognizable. As far as she could remember, she had never visited the farm nor seen the interior of the house. Except for the photo on her father's study wall and the stories her grandmother had told her during those infrequent visits more than eight years ago, she had had no knowledge of the house or the people in it. And yet, since she had first entered Auntie's room, she had had a sense of being in place, of being chosen to share in some intimate, still unrevealed secret. It was a disquieting sensation, exaggerated by her sense of being watched by shadowy, unseen, and unknown observers.

"It's this house. It's full of tricks," she said to herself, trying to shake the prickly feeling on the back of her neck. "First voices, now faces."

Once again she turned slowly before the mirror, looking all around, waiting for the warm, hospitable atmosphere to surround her as it had the day before. Instead the room felt chilly, as though it reflected her own fears and apprehensions.

"How is it, Amy? My goodness!" Grandma exclaimed. "Why, you look exactly like a colonial girl. If we braid your hair and pin it up, you'll look like you just stepped out of a history book."

Amy flounced the skirt over her petticoats. "It pokes me around the waist."

"Be glad you don't have to wear stays and a corset the way we did at your age." Deftly her fingers plaited Amy's long brown hair and wound the braids at the back of her head. "There. All you need now is the cap."

Amy looked in the mirror. The two faces she had seen before seemed to have merged, her own transformed by the dress and hair style into that of a child of another time. Her own nose, her own eyes, her own jaw were reflected in the mirror, exact down to the chicken pox scar above her right eye. And the curious gaze was definitely her own. Yet the familiar young woman she saw was also a stranger. Clothed in the past,

Amy became in that moment someone she had not yet met, the colonial *doppelgänger* of her twentieth-century self. To shake off the eerie sensation, Amy turned her back on the mirror and quickly followed her grandmother out of the room to fetch her colonial cap.

After breakfast Amy and Grandma gathered the boxes of preserves and waited with Auntie on the porch for their ride to church. The old woman nodded approvingly at Amy's costume but did not remark on it. She seemed distant from them as though her mind, like her eyesight, moved in and out of focus between abrupt, blank lapses. At quarter to ten a wagon drawn by a pair of bored, long-eared mules clattered up Bridge Street and into the driveway.

"Sorry to be late, ladies, but these two critters don't think that they should have to work on Sunday." A tall, middle-aged man in a powdered wig and blue velvet breeches climbed down from the wagon seat and hitched the reins around the porch railing.

"That's all right, Mr. Winters," Grandma said. "We appreciate your coming to get us at all. You haven't met my granddaughter, Amy Enfield. She'll be staying with us for a time. Amy, shake hands with Mr. Winters."

"How do you do, Amy." He took her hand and bowed over it, in keeping with his costume. "Climb up in the wagon there next to Betsy. Looks like she's finally got a neighbor her own age."

A small, rounded face peeked out from behind the wagon seat. As Mr. Winters helped Auntie up into the wagon, his daughter's eyes widened. She scrambled to the rear of the wagon bed and crouched there, staring at Auntie's back. Amy clambered up the wheel spokes, awkward in her long skirts, and nodded shyly at Betsy, but the child just shook her head and pointed surreptitiously at the old lady. When the preserves were loaded, Grandma climbed in, surprisingly agile, and sat beside the girls. The wheels crunched on the gravel, and the wagon started back down Bridge Street.

"How are you this morning, Betsy?"

"Fine, Mrs. Enfield." Her voice was barely audible, and she glanced quickly back and forth from Grandma to where Auntie sat in the wagon seat next to Mr. Winters.

"Have you and your brother been doing any more exploring lately?" Grandma's eyes twinkled, but her face was stern.

"Oh, no, ma'am!" Betsy blushed deep red beneath her tan. "We wouldn't do that, not again."

"I should hope not! You're all ready for the Fair?"

"I'm doing one of the tours this year." Her blush faded and Betsy looked at Amy. "Would you like to help out?"

"Of course she would," Grandma answered for her. "We'll be there all afternoon."

"I just wish we didn't have to go in this old mule wagon." Betsy's face screwed up into a scowl. "What a way to go to church."

"Your ancestors didn't mind. It's better than shank's mare." Mr. Winters slowed the wagon. "I'm sure Henry and Sam wouldn't object to a lighter load, if you'd like to walk."

"Oh, Daddy," Betsy groaned. She watched the mules' ears flop as the animals slowed to a walk. "We must look ridiculous."

"The church has been having this Fair for so many years, no one thinks these getups are odd. We don't look any more ridiculous than he does, for instance." Mr. Winters saluted the bewigged driver of a 1939 Pontiac as it passed, then turned onto the main highway. Other cars passed them, with children pointing and waving from rear windows. Amy and Betsy waved back, sheepishly at first, as the wagon moved slowly down the narrow, winding road. Here, on the outskirts of town, the houses were far apart and built close up to the thorough-fare. White-shingled with green or black shutters, their roofs sloping to carry the weight of snow through a New England winter, these were comfortable, solid dwellings, well suited to the rolling countryside. The fields around them were not the easily farmed, rich soil of Amy's experience, but were rock-strewn, uneven acres. Years of spring plowing had cleared many of the larger stones, which formed the fences along the road and between the farms. But the larger boulders remained, exposed heart of the mountains themselves, and in these fields the cows and horses grazed. And on all sides, the soft hills rose in graded shades of color, cresting in the rounded summits of the Berkshires. Just looking at their sweep across the horizon gave Amy a sense of peace. She was sorry for the ride to end when Mr. Winters turned off at the church.

He guided the wagon into the churchyard and tied the mules to a hitching post left over from the days before auto-mobiles. After lifting Auntie down from the wagon, he helped Grandma unload the preserves. All the parishioners were out-side, setting up the tables and booths for the Fair. Betsy and Amy watched from the church steps with Auntie.

"How come you're staying here?" Betsy asked.

"It's just until my parents get settled. We're moving to Chicago."

Betsy glanced at Auntie, who was leaning on her cane in the hot sun, then pulled Amy a little to one side. "I'll bet you hate it," she whispered. "That's a spooky old house."

"And why should it be spooky?" Auntie turned to face them. "You're still trying to stir things up, aren't you? Well, just because I'm old doesn't mean I'm completely deaf, young lady. Mind your manners or I'll give you another lesson in behavior. You, child, help me inside. Better you should learn some history than to stand out here listening to idle gossip."

Her grip was strong on Amy's arm, steering the girl into the dim, empty church. It was a small building with pews in the center and two side aisles. Each row of pews had a door which, before central heating, had helped to keep the cold drafts off the parishioners' feet. There were stained-glass windows, a gallery upstairs for the choir, and two marble tablets on each side of the chancel. The one on the right listed the important dates in the church's history, and on the left was a list of the rectors of the church.

₁ "People have been worshipping in this spot since 1648, when the first meeting house was built on this land," Auntie said. "Of course, the church was built much later. Those pillars reach from cellar to ceiling, cut from single trees they are. And this was Philo Coburn's pew." Her gnarled hand felt for the latch, turned it, and opened the pew door. "It wasn't always this fancy. There weren't any Tiffany glass windows back then, and no marble plaques, nor people who thought they could change history by crossing it out."

Amy sat down on the red velvet cushion and looked around. The church smelled of candles and old wood and bore the respectful hush of age as well as of prayer. She sank into it as she might have submerged herself in a cool lake on a hot summer day, letting the two hundred and some years of the past ripple around her.

"You see that tablet on the left, the list of rectors?"

Amy squinted to make out the chiseled letters. "It's too dark. I can't see the words."

" 'Resigned,' it says, resigned in good standing after each one had served St. George's." Auntie snorted. "Resigned indeed! There's one that never resigned from this church. Philo Coburn fixed his wagon, all right. Drove the Tory rector out, the townspeople did, and lucky they didn't tar and feather him to boot. He was removed from this parish by his own congregation and shot dead later for the loyalist coward he was. Removed from this parish he'd have been for all time if some namby-pamby vestryman hadn't had the stonecutter alter the record." She clutched her cane with both hands, then swung it to nudge Amy in the shins. "You come to church to pray, child. My old knees won't stand the strain, but yours surely will."

The church began to fill, Grandma joined them, and soon the service began. Although it was cool and pleasant in the church, the scent of burning candles mingling with that of newly mown grass in the churchyard, the air pressed heavily on Amy's skin. She shifted uncomfortably in the straight-backed pew and sagged on the kneeling pad during the prayers of intercession. Even Auntie's occasional sharp prodding could not keep her attentive to the service. If she closed her eyes in an effort to concentrate, waves of sleep pounded in her ears, beating down her consciousness. But when she stood up and tried to join with the congregation in the prayers and responses, the air seemed too thin to support her breath. It was simultaneously oppressive and devoid of oxygen, as though some giant pump were removing that vital gas as it increased the pressure on Amy's lungs. When the rector mounted the pulpit to begin his sermon, he seemed to Amy to move slowly through a thickening atmosphere, like a deep-sea diver at half speed, distant as the tolling of an underwater bell. The words made no sense to her, ringing out in nonsense rhymes. She shook her head and took a deep breath, leaning toward the aisle. Of its own volition the latch at her fingertips turned, the door popped open, and Amy nearly fell out on the floor.

"Sit still, child," Auntie hissed. "Close the door and sit still."

She tried to pull the door to, but it resisted. She rose slightly from her seat and yanked. As suddenly as it had sprung open, the door slammed shut, and Amy fell backward with a thump. The rector paused in his sermon, looked up at her over his half glasses, then continued. The spell was broken. Amy heard him quite clearly now. She twisted the peg and secured the door once more.

"Are you feeling all right, Amy?" Grandma asked after the service. "You look a little pale."

"I'm all right. Everything seemed to slow down all of a sudden. I'm sorry about the door."

"You just need some fresh air and a cool drink. Come and sit down at the table. You can help sell the preserves."

"I'll be along in a minute, Grandma. I want to find Betsy." Amy lingered in the vestibule of the church. While the parishioners filed out, she read the brass plaque tacked to the plain, dark wood table. It was the original communion table, smooth and hollowed slightly on top, warm with sunlight from the open door. Above it was hung a glass-enclosed parchment, the charter granted to the church by King George himself in 1735. Through the open door Amy could see the costumed parishioners moving around the tables set up on the lawn. The rector, in a black frock coat, breeches, and white stockings, mingled with them as his predecessor might have done two hundred years ago. The scene had a dreamlike quality, as though Amy were looking through a window into the past.

Suddenly the wind picked up, scattering dried leaves from the trees, catching in the long full skirts of the colonial ladies. With a rush it swirled across the church steps and caught at the heavy oak doors. They creaked, then slowly swung shut, blocking Amy's view and leaving her in darkness, blinded by the change in light. She remained with her hand on the table, motionless in the dim stillness. The small room closed around her as a thunderstorm closes on a summer night, charged with the coming clash of atmospheric forces, yet utterly still. Then, as if from a great distance, she heard the creak of floorboards inside the church. Amy backed away from the table, feeling behind her for the wrought-iron latch of the outside doors. Her fingers touched the cool metal as a rush of dry, musty air burst from the interior of the church. A dark figure appeared beside the communion table, its white face glowing out of the shadows. Amy gasped and stepped back, pressing down on the latch.

IV

Hallowed Ground

As easily as it had closed, the door swung open. Sunlight pierced the interior of the vestibule, washing out all color. In that first instant of brightness, light and darkness were reversed the way a streak of lightning bleaches out rain-blackened tree trunks. Like a photo negative the figure appeared translucent beside the communion table, its face now a black void above gleaming silvery vestments. The vision lasted only seconds; Amy blinked, color returned, and she saw a man standing before her in a long black robe, a wide white tie at his throat. He reached out toward her, murmuring inaudibly. Amy pressed back against the door, still clutching the latch.

"Dear child," he began in a rusty whisper, "have you returned to me at last? I've waited so long. I thought I had lost you."

Amy glanced behind her, looking for the person he addressed, but there was no one.

"Can it be you know me not?" His lips moved stiffly. "Has time so altered these features that they fire no recognition in you? Yet in your face I see that same sweet child of my heart's youth. Look upon me!" His hollow voice rose in pitch and he stretched out both hands. "Come to me, I beg you, and repair the bond which time has sorely weakened. Restore the heart your faithlessness has broken. Come!"

Amy wanted to turn and run out into the sunshine of the churchyard, away from this strange man, but the pleading in his voice, his outstretched hands, held her back.

"Speak to me," he said, his voice stronger now. "Tell me at least how I have failed you. If love is gone, let knowledge be my solace. Return to me the charge I left you, fulfill our broken covenant, and I will go. Speak to me."

"I don't know who you think I am," Amy stuttered, clinging to the door. "But you've got me mixed up with someone else. I'm new here. My name is Amy, Amy Enfield."

"There is no Enfield in my parish." The man stared at her, his face darkening in a frown. "Betray me if you must, but compound not your action with lies. Remember, this is the house of God."

"I'm not lying," Amy insisted. "I'm here visiting my grandmother. Ask her if you don't believe me."

"What have they done to you that you should deny me so?" His voice softened. "Have no fear of me, my child, forgiveness is at hand. Come."

"I'm not denying anybody." Amy edged toward the open porch of the church. "And I'm not your child. I'm Amy Enfield."

"And yet you bear her face. I do not understand." His hands dropped to his sides and he stared at her. His face was troubled, bewildered. Quite suddenly he seemed more vulnerable than threatening.

"Are you sure you're in the right place?" Amy's fear gave way to concern. Perhaps he was the village eccentric, his hold on reality weakened by the costumes and activities of the Fair, an odd but not dangerous individual. "Maybe you're lost. Let me take you to the rector. He'll help you."

"The rector? Have you lost your senses, child? I am the rector. Under siege in my own church, it's true, but my own church it is. If the townsfolk find me here, they'll tar and feather me for a traitor, misguided though they be. Seek you no one else!"

"Tar and feather? No one would do that." Amy's thoughts went reeling back to Auntie's lecture in the church. "Not anymore they wouldn't. Besides, you can't be the rector. The rector gave the sermon." Amy looked closely at him. He appeared to be younger than the man she had seen in the pulpit, though his face was haggard and lined. "Are you the assistant?"

"I am the rector. I built this church, baptized its children, and buried its dead, your brothers among them. Have you forgotten the price your father paid for his politics? His own sons killed in the conflict he supported. Have you forgotten so easily?" He looked around him, at the historical plaques on the church wall and on the communion table. Gently he touched the worn dark wood. "What have they done to my church? Have they replaced me, then? This traitorous parish defies both God and his royal servant." He focused again on Amy, his black gaze pinning her at the door. "The silver," he demanded, his voice an agitated whisper. "They have not found the silver?"

"Silver? What silver?"

"Beware. You stand on holy ground. Speak the truth lest you damn yourself by the words of your own mouth." His eyes glowed darkly. "Have you become one of them that you would try to trick me? Everyone knows of the silver, the gift of the Crown to her church in the New World. The rebels have not found it? It remains well hidden?"

"What rebels? I really don't know what you're talking about." Amy was beginning to be alarmed again by the interrogation of this stranger. "I don't know anything about your old silver."

"Not mine, but given in trust by the Queen, kept safe, I pray, from the hands of these traitors to the Crown."

"We have no queen. This is the United States of America."

"Can it be you speak the truth? You know nothing of the gifts of Queen Anne, the chalice and paten sent by Her Grace that her people might partake of the Holy Sacrament?"

Amy shook her head.

"But this is the Church of England, by order of King George the Third."

"No," Amy said, recalling facts and dates from her American history. "No, it is the Episcopal Church, and the only King George is George the Sixth of England, and he has no Queen Anne."

"George the Sixth?" For a moment the man simply stared at her. Then his shoulders sagged and his face crumpled. Incredulously he held his hands palm up before him, a frozen study in black and white. His pale face and hands seemed less distinct, and his black robe ebbed and blended with the dark shadows of the vestibule. "I understand," he said at last, his voice deep with grief. "The rebels have had their way. You are not the one whom I seek. But if you would aid a troubled soul, find her. Only she can fulfill my trust."

"What trust? Who is she?" Amy stepped toward him.

"Find her. I cannot rest until my mission is complete." He backed away from the table.

"Wait," Amy protested, reaching out to him as he disappeared into the church. She darted across the vestibule after him. "Wait. Stop."

But the white-doored pews were vacant, the aisles and chancel empty and still. The altar had been cleared, the candles extinguished, and only the moted sunlight occupied the silent church.

"Were you talking to me?"

Amy whirled around. Entering the church behind her was a boy about her own age, still dressed in the red cassock of the crucifer and carrying the heavy silver cross that led the choir into and out of the church before and after the service.

"Where did he go," she asked, "that man in the black robe? Did you see him?"

"There's nobody out there in a black robe." He hefted the cross and started down the aisle. "I just came in to put this in the sacristy. What did he look like?"

"He was tall, taller than you, with silver blond hair." Amy followed the boy. "And he had on a long black robe with a white tie. You couldn't help noticing him."

"The way everyone's dressed up, he'd fit right in. He doesn't sound familiar."

"I met him right here in the church. He said he was the rector."

"The rector's in the churchyard."

"You must know this man. He's a little strange. He kept talking about the queen's silver. He acted really funny."

The boy stopped, turned slowly, and looked at her. "He asked about some silver?"

"Yes. You know about it? Who is he, anyway, the village eccentric?"

Holding the cross between them, the boy stared at Amy. "You're new here, aren't you? You're the girl who fell out of the pew."

"I'm visiting my grandmother. Tell me about the silver. Is something missing from the church?"

"No, no, it's nothing."

"And the man? He's not dangerous, is he?"

"I haven't seen him." He stepped back. "I've got to get changed."

"He'd be hard to miss, the way he acts."

The boy shrugged and started to turn away, then paused. "Where did you say you were staying?"

"With my grandmother, at the old Griffin place. I'm Amy Enfield."

"I'm Ben Winters." He waited, looking at her with a curious expression, as though he expected a reaction to his name.

"You're Betsy's brother? I met her this morning."

"Did she tell you anything? About your family, I mean."

Amy shook her head. "She started to, but Auntie interrupted. My grandmother asked if you'd been doing any more exploring. What's that about?"

"Just take my advice and don't go digging around that house. They don't like it. And forget about that old guy and his silver. It's nothing."

"You do know him, don't you?"

"Listen, I've got to go."

"Wait." Amy touched his arm. "At least tell me who he is."

"I said I don't know." He pulled away from her, picked up the cross, and hurried down the aisle into the sacristy. Amy stared after him, then turned and ran out of the church.

"Grandma," she began as she bounded breathlessly up to the table where the two women sat. "Grandma, have you seen a man with blond hair and a long black robe? He says he's the rector."

"Calm down, Amy. You'll make yourself faint again. Sit down here and have something cool to drink. That's better." She poured a glass of apple cider and handed it to Amy. "The rector was just here, buying his annual supply of strawberry jam. How that man loves my preserves! But he's in breeches and a frock coat, over there with the powdered wig on. I swear he enjoys this Fair more than the children do."

"Then it must be another rector. He's younger, with a sad face and a funny way of talking."

"There is only one rector, dear," Grandma said. "We couldn't afford an assistant for such a small parish. It was probably one of the townspeople."

Amy glanced around the churchyard, looking for the black and white costume. Most of the men were in breeches and long stockings, though a few wore overalls and wide-brimmed farmers' hats. The man in the church was nowhere in sight.

"You must know who he is," Amy insisted. "He mistook me for someone else, someone he's been looking for. He even accused me of lying about my name. He's very odd. Do I look like someone else?"

Auntie regarded Amy from behind her glasses. "The Griffin bones," she said, nodding slowly. "You've got the Griffin bones, passed down from Lucy herself."

"Yes, there is a family likeness," Grandma agreed, as she stopped arranging her jars of preserves and considered Amy. "Especially now that you're dressed in the colonial clothes. But no one here would mistake you for our Lucy Griffin."

"There's none alive today who'd recognize her unless he'd seen the portrait."

"Who was he, then?" Amy asked again.

"Those Winters children were up to the house," Auntie muttered. "They might have seen the portrait."

"Now, Matilda, what would they know of Lucy Griffin? He must be one of the parishioners."

"But he was so upset," Amy said, scanning the churchyard. "He seemed really confused."

"No need for you to take on his problems, child. There's plenty enough to keep you busy in your own family. It's time we planted those mums. The sun's not quite so strong now. Here, child, take that box of plants and give me your arm." Auntie rose from the chair, and, leaning on her cane, clutched Amy's arm with her free hand. "You mind the table, Louise. We can do it."

. Despite her failing sight, Auntie led Amy easily across the open churchyard and into the old section of graves near the church. The older stones were of red sandstone, washed clean of name and scripture by years of weather. Here and there a marker of white granite tilted up, the name and date still legible. They passed family plots, one fenced off from its neighbors by iron barriers, the patriarch immortalized beneath an angel-topped monument. Here Auntie paused for a moment.

"Even in death they set themselves above the rest of us," she said, "for all the good it did them. Charles wasn't so bad, but those sons of his should have been fenced off from good, God-fearing people while they lived, not after they went to meet their Maker. Still, they got their just deserts. One of them was childless, the other two had only daughters. It's Lucy's son that bore the name and passed it on."

Amy looked up to where the name Griffin was chiseled in block letters on the monument. Beside it a row of smaller stones marked the graves of the three sons and their father. Auntie tugged on Amy's arm and led her to the very edge of the churchyard.

"They buried Lucy over here, near her father, and the rest of the family after her. There, that flat white stone is hers."

Amy set down the mums and read from the stone. "Lucy," it said, "relict of Charles Griffin, died June 28, 1839. How's her name in the sight of God."

"Her son always complained about that stone," Auntie said. "But Lucy insisted upon it, even before she died. Had it put in her will, she did, and he didn't dare go against her."

"What does it mean? What's a relict?"

"A relict's a widow, one who's left behind. It's an old-fashioned term. As for the words, I guess poor Lucy was worried about his judgment on her, though why I can't imagine. She was a good soul, from all I've heard." Auntie slipped a pair of scissors from her pocket and handed them to Amy. "Here, cut off the dahlia stems, and we'll put the mums in around the stone."

Amy did as she was directed, setting the mum plants in bunches around the white marker, pressing the black earth tight around them. Her aunt leaned on the cane, watching as though she could indeed see where Amy placed each plant. There was something uncanny about her sight, a wilfulness in it, in when she saw and when she didn't. It would have been no surprise to Amy if the old woman could see through walls as well as windows, recognize people a mile away as easily as she recognized them by the touch of her cold, bony fingers. Auntie looked across the slope of the graveyard and up the hill.

"Philo Coburn chose this site because it's in view of the house. You can see the elm from here, on a line with the one in the meadow behind the church, just as if they'd been planted on a plumb line from the church steeple."

Amy stood up and brushed off her hands. The two trees and the steeple rose like three points on a diagonal line up the hill toward the house. The meadow grass was brown, touched with green and yellow spikes of goldenrod and black-eyed Susan, and the leaves of the trees were tinged with brown. The breeze blew gently, clouds shifted in a blue sky, a flash of color showed as a pair of red-winged blackbirds burst from the field in search of swampier hunting grounds. For perhaps the first time in her life, Amy was aware of her sight and as suddenly aware of the loss her great-aunt suffered. "Do you see at all, Auntie," she asked quietly, "or do you just remember?"

"Remembering is seeing, child." Auntie looked down at the gravestone again. "Now, go and fetch some water. The plants will need a drink. I'll wait on you here."

"That man I saw, do you remember him?"

"I'd not waste my memory or my sight on the likes of him," Auntie snapped. "There's some would play such a poor joke on you, child. No doubt that Winters boy and his sister are up to something again. You attend to your business. Fetch that water now, before the plants wilt. No, not that way," she said, catching Amy's arm as the girl started back through the cemetery to the booths on the church lawn. "Go around the other side of the fence. It's shorter, and you won't have to disturb twice those souls laid in hallowed ground."

Amy left her leaning on the cane by Lucy's stone and climbed over the stone fence into the field that ran behind the church. She swung through the long grasses, her skirt catching in clumps of milkweed and Queen Anne's lace.

"It certainly isn't any shorter," she said to herself, tripping through hillocks of meadow grass. "And a lot rougher than through the churchyard." She reached the far corner of the church, shaded by the elm in the field, and turned to climb back over the low fence. A large rock lay at the base of the tree. Amy bent to pick it up, intending to place it back on the wall from which she assumed it had fallen. Tilting it up, she brushed the earth from its underside, looking at the curious pattern of crevices. Like a graphite rubbing, the marks caught the dirt, formed into letters, and became clear. Hand-cut in the stone was the date 1783, and the words Seth Howes, Rector.

V

Seth Howes

Amy thrust the rough-hewn block out of her hands and stumbled backward into the low stone wall that marked the boundary of the church property. She stared down at the tombstone, both fascinated and repelled. An indentation at the base of the tree showed where it had lain for over a century, dislodged accidentally by some burrowing animal or by the traffic of the neighborhood children who played in the meadow. But what was it doing here, on the wrong side of the fence? Surely the rector of the church would be buried in the churchyard. Hesitantly Amy stepped away from the wall and knelt in front of the gravestone, inspecting the crudely chiseled inscription. "Seth Howes, Rector," she read again, "Died, 1783."

Amy tried to visualize the list of rectors on the marble tablet in the church. Hadn't Auntie said there was one who didn't belong, one who did not resign but was removed? Certainly the date was right for this to be the outcast Tory rector, the loyalist rejected by his Yankee parish. Removed from his church by the people he served, had he also been denied the solace of burial in the hallowed ground of his own churchyard? Amy was touched with sadness. Gently she traced the letters of his name in the rough stone, as though that human contact could pass through death and time itself to erase the dead man's judgment. At least she could replace the stone that marked his grave and leave him in peace once more. Amy lifted the heavy chunk of granite and set it back beneath the tree, recalling suddenly her conversation with the man in the church. In vivid fragments, portions of their brief encounter tumbled about in Amy's mind, colliding with her reason and her belief in the laws of nature. Everything about that grim-faced individual —his bearing, his clothes, his speech—typified a time long past, a time honored for one week each year as an anniversary celebration by the people of St. George's. He claimed to be the rector of a rebellious parish, a parish that had defied God's royal servant, George the Third. Anyone who had studied history could have said those things, Amy reminded herself, trying to explain the mysterious figure. But he had also recognized Amy as the ancestor she resembled, the Lucy Griffin whose brothers he had buried, casualties of the rebellion he opposed. In a dry, chilling echo, Auntie's words repeated themselves, mingling with the soft rush of wind through the meadow grasses.

"There's none alive today would recognize her. . . ."

Slowly Amy stood up and eased out of the shadow of the great elm. Seth Howes was dead. He had been dead for over one hundred fifty years, and his bones lay crumbling beneath the old elm, acknowledged only by the rough piece of rock she had stumbled upon. Seth Howes was dead, yet she had seen and talked with him.

"It isn't possible." Amy shivered, pressing her cold hands against the sun-warmed rocks of the stone wall, then snatching them away to stare at her palms in horror. Stooping, she scrubbed her hands against the soft brown meadow grass until the last trace of dirt from the tombstone was gone.

"I don't believe in ghosts," she murmured. "I don't. He looked too real. I could have reached out and touched him." Again a shiver chilled through her, raising the hair on the back of her neck. If she had reached out to that black gown, if she had grasped the arm of the departing figure, would his being have shrunk like fog from her mortal touch? Or would she have been drawn with him into that vaporous existence of time past? Amy shuddered, then straightened slowly, forcing herself to think rationally. She had been alone in the vestibule. The figure had appeared and then vanished into the church proper. Moments later Ben had entered from the vestibule claiming he had seen no one.

"But there are no such things as ghosts," she repeated aloud. If I had touched it, she thought, I probably would have felt a flesh and blood twentieth-century arm as real as my own, as real as—Ben's. Her suspicion came suddenly, logically. Auntie had warned her about Ben and Betsy.

"It must be a trick, just as Auntie said. Ben and Betsy must be teasing me."

"Amy? Amy, I've been looking all over for you." Betsy Winters stood at the opposite side of the fence, looking curiously at Amy's pale face. "What's the matter?"

"You tell me." Amy's voice came out more harshly than she intended. She cleared her throat and clambered over the wall. In the presence of another human being the meadow and its grave resumed their natural proportions, the shadow of Seth Howes's death lifting from them as though a cloud had shifted past the face of the sun. Even the figure in the church had lost some of its mystery, so sure was Amy that a prank had been played upon her. Her recovery from the fright was tinged with anger.

"If you and Ben wanted to scare me," she said, "you really

succeeded. And I don't think it's very funny. What is it? An initiation rite of friendship I had to pass?"

Betsy glanced from Amy to the flat stone beneath the elm tree. "So you found his grave, too. But Ben and I didn't have anything to do with that. We didn't try to scare you. I came to see if you wanted to come on the tour. Your grandmother said it was all right."

"You can start the tour right now. Who's Seth Howes?"

"He was the rector of the church during the Revolutionary War. And he's buried here, under the elm."

"That much I figured out on my own. I mean the man in the church. He must be someone from the village, a descendant or something."

"Seth Howes had no descendants. I read all about him. The book said he was 'relieved of his duties' when the Americans drove the British out of town. He was killed a week later and buried here. But nobody remembers that. They didn't like him much." Betsy paused, her round face serious, as though Amy's question had just registered. "What man in the church?"

"The man you planted there to act like Seth Howes. He said he was the rector and kept asking me about some silver. Ben said he never heard of him, but he wasn't very convincing. Come on, Betsy, who's the man I talked to?"

"You talked to Seth Howes about the silver?" Betsy's brown eyes grew rounder in her small face. "He's dead. You couldn't have."

"Of course I couldn't have. So who was he? And why did Ben lie about knowing him? Unless the man in the church was Ben, or someone you two set up to scare me. Auntie warned me about your tricks."

"Amy, honestly, we didn't pull any tricks on you. Not that

I know of. Ben might have done it as a joke, but he wouldn't lie about knowing the man."

Betsy's sincerity was unquestionable. She returned Amy's gaze evenly, without wavering, her head held high, her chin set, ready to defend her innocence. For a moment the two girls looked at one another. Then Amy smiled.

"I'm sorry," she said. "It seemed more logical, and not as frightening, to blame you and Ben than to think that I'd seen a ...." Amy paused, swallowed, and filled in the word. "Than to think that I'd seen a spirit. But who could the man have been? What else do you know about Seth Howes?"

Betsy hiked herself up on the stone wall. "I don't know who you saw in the church or what he knows about the silver. All I know about Seth Howes I read in the rector's history books, and anyone could do that. When Seth Howes was driven out of the church, he took the communion silver with him. He was killed before he could get to the British lines, but the silver was never found. Ben and I think he hid it somewhere, and we're going to find it."

"The chalice and paten Queen Anne gave to the church? That man asked me if anyone had found them."

Betsy frowned. "No one's thought of that silver for years, as far as I know. Most of the parishioners don't even know it existed."

"The whole town will know now." Ben approached them across the church lawn, glaring at his sister. "Betsy, can't you ever keep your mouth shut? Everybody will be looking for the silver before you're finished."

"You're the one who tried to scare her, you and your weird jokes, pretending to be Seth Howes. It's your fault."

"You really had me convinced I was seeing things," Amy added, "but you can stop acting now. You had to be the man in the church."

"Sure," Ben nodded, running his fingers through his deep auburn hair. "I ran out of the church as Seth Howes, unbleached my hair, changed my clothes, shrank a couple of inches, and came back in behind you. It wasn't me."

"But whoever it was knows about the silver. He told me all about it."

"And as long as she already knows," Betsy said, "we might as well work together. Three heads are better than two."

"Especially when one of the two is yours." Ben frowned. "It's too late now. I'd sure like to know if someone else is in on this."

"Maybe it isn't some*one* else," Betsy whispered. "Maybe it's some*thing* else. What exactly did he say, Amy?"

Quickly Amy related all she could remember of her conversation. "He seemed so confused," she concluded, "as though he didn't know where he was. He kept accusing me of lying to him about the silver. Do you suppose he's crazy?"

"Now we can choose between a ghost and a nut," Ben mocked. "Come on, Amy, I'll bet your aunt told you all about Seth Howes. You're just making up the character in the church so you can horn in on our hunt."

"I didn't know anything about your hunt," Amy snapped, offended in her turn at Ben's accusation. "That's how you got into trouble, isn't it, poking around the Griffin house without permission."

"We weren't poking around," Ben said, his face reddening. "We were doing research. You see, Betsy read this book that told about Seth Howes taking the silver."

"I told her that," Betsy interrupted. "And it said that because people here thought he was a traitor they wouldn't bury him in the churchyard. Ben and I looked around and sure enough, we found his grave, out here under the elm."

"We figured that he'd have hidden the silver somewhere close to the church, so we decided to explore."

"And Auntie saw you."

Ben and Betsy looked at each other. "Not the way you mean," Ben said. "She just knew we were there."

"Until then I never really believed what they said in the village about your aunt and her second sight," Betsy added.

"Second sight?" Amy asked.

Betsy's eyes shifted away from Amy to focus on the stone fence. "You just came here. You haven't heard the stories we grew up on. And I'm not trying to scare you." She glanced back at Amy. "The old folks in the village say that if your aunt had lived in Salem, she would have been burned as a witch."

"She is a bit peculiar, and she's old and can't see very well, but I'd hardly call her a witch," Amy said. She wanted no verification of her suspicions about Auntie's sight.

"I'm only telling you what they say. And it isn't just because she's old. She's always been able to see things, things other people can't see."

Amy forced aside the image of Auntie's blank, knowing eyes. "That's just town gossip. You mean she caught you and Ben where you weren't supposed to be."

Betsy shook her head. "She knew where we were."

"And where, exactly, was that?"

"Look." Ben picked up a small piece of soft chalkstone and bent over the fence. On one of the flat rocks he began to sketch a crude map. "We're here, on the edge of the church-yard. The land directly behind the church was part of the original charter from the king. The rectory used to be up toward the top of the hill, to the left of your grandmother's house. It burned or fell down years ago and was never rebuilt because it was so far from town. The church bought another place for the rectory. Anyway, your land and the church's are separated from the town by a small stream, here." He drew a crooked line down the side of the rock.

"We know from the record that Howes ran away from the settlement, which means he probably headed up into the hills," Betsy went on. "Perhaps he even stopped at the rectory to pick up his things, if he had time. Then we figured he would have gone south to New York, where the British headquarters were."

"But he didn't make it." Ben tapped the chalk on his map. "He must have hid somewhere around here, and there's a good chance he left the silver where he was holed up. So Betsy and I started up through the field behind the church toward the stream. We thought there might be a cave up there, someplace where he could have camped."

"Do you realize how long ago that was?" Amy exclaimed. "It would have fallen down by now or be all overgrown."

Ben glanced at her in disgust. "You think we didn't think of that? We've been playing in these hills all our lives and we never found anything. But this time we were looking."

"And you found something?"

"Not exactly." Betsy shook her head. "But there's a place where the stream widens, a sort of pond with rocks tumbled all around it."

"With stepping stones across and a flat boulder in the center," Amy burst out. The words came not at her volition, but in description of a vivid, brilliant image that flashed in her mind with the clarity of a photograph.

"So you've been exploring, too," Ben said.

"No, I haven't been there." Amy felt somewhat bewildered. The image had been so clear, and rimmed with words not her own, as though a distant radio transmitter had found a speaker in her mind. She shook off the impression. "I must have seen a picture of it somewhere. I'll bet my father fished that stream."

"At first we thought Howes might have sunk the silver in the water," Betsy continued. "Maybe there's a spring farther up, or an opening in the rocks. And then we noticed the birch grove."

"It wouldn't have been there in Seth Howes's time. The trees would have been small, like bushes, so you could have seen the Griffin barn among them, the old stone one in the back." Ben tossed his chalk away and sat on the fence. "It seemed as likely a place as any. We weren't going to hurt anything, just look around. There's nothing in the barn anyway, not since your family stopped farming the place. Find a loose stone in the foundation and bingo! The silver."

"So that's where Auntie found you. No wonder she was angry."

Again the brother and sister exchanged glances. Finally Betsy spoke. "She didn't find us there. She was waiting for us, waiting inside the barn."

"But that's ridiculous. Why would she do that?" Amy asked. "Maybe she just wanted something from the barn and happened to be there. Though I can't imagine her going herself. She'd send Grandma. She has enough trouble getting around, between her poor eyesight and her arthritis."

"She was there all right," Ben said. "We opened the barn door and there she was. Darn near broke my shin with that cane of hers. And was she mad! She marched us right off to your grandmother and told her she'd found us snooping around. She acted as though we'd made off with the family jewels."

"It wasn't that bad, Ben." Betsy turned to Amy. "Your grandmother got her calmed down and sent us home. She was really nice about it, but told us not to come back, that it upset your aunt."

"Did you tell Auntie about your research?"

"Betsy tried to, but she said we had no business involving her family with the likes of Seth Howes. I tell you, she knew where we'd been and was waiting for us."

"She does have a thing about family history." Suddenly Amy remembered the mums, and her aunt standing in the hot sun awaiting her return with the water. "I've got to get back to her. Walk with me as far as the tables."

The three started across the churchyard together, musing over Seth Howes. Suddenly Amy stopped.

"You know, the way Auntie talks about the Griffin family, they'd have been the last people in town to shelter a Tory. Her great-grandfather hated the British. I doubt that old Seth would have hung around their barn! And if he was going to retrieve the silver before he joined the British, and if he was killed the night he left, the silver must be hidden near where he died."

Ben nodded slowly. "That's a lot of ifs, Amy, but you could be right. He wouldn't have been carrying the silver around with him. It was probably the last thing he'd pick up on his way south. So if it wasn't on him when he died, it must still be hidden where he left it. Did any of the books mention whose property he was on, or who killed him?"

Betsy assumed her tour guide posture. "He was shot by one of the townspeople who thought he was a British spy or renegade. After all, there was a war on, and this good Yankee wasn't going to have his barn raided by some no-good Redcoat."

"Save the speech for the paying customers," Ben said, "and tell us who the hero was who shot him. Maybe that's the barn we should look in."

"It was some funny name. One of those old-fashioned ones, like Asa or Philomenus or ...."

"Or Philo? Philo Coburn?"

"How did you know?" Betsy looked at Amy in amazement.

"He's Auntie's great-grandfather. She told me that he

fixed Seth Howes's wagon, but I never thought she meant that. How terrible." Amy stood still, staring out over the meadow, chilled once more by the hate that had destroyed Seth Howes. "I've got to go," she said abruptly, gathering up her skirts in order to run more easily. "I'll see you later. I've got to talk to Auntie."

VI

St. George's Fair

The names of her ancestors rang in Amy's ears as she raced across the churchyard. Philo Coburn, Lucy Griffin, Seth Howes —like the cadence of a drum roll the syllables of their names beat in time to her footsteps. With a quick explanation to her grandmother, she snatched a bottle and filled it from the tap by the church, splashing and slopping water over the graves as she ran back across the church grounds to Lucy Griffin's grave site. Auntie was standing still, bent forward on her cane, her lips moving in a steady murmur. Before Amy could make out what she was saying, the old woman turned, saw her, and straightened up.

"Took you long enough, child. When I was your age, I was faster on my feet than that. Pour the water on now, and get me back to my chair. These old legs can't take so much standing."

"Auntie?" Breathless from her run, Amy gulped for air as she poured the water over the newly set plants. "Auntie, what did you say happened to that rector, the one who was removed from the church?"

"Philo Coburn shot him, which is better than he deserved. A good hanging would have sufficed."

"What difference does it make now?" Amy protested, startled at Auntie's vehemence. "That was so long ago."

"Has time made Benedict Arnold any less of a traitor? Seth Howes was no better."

"Did he really steal something from the church?"

"There's some that called it stealing, man of the cloth though he was. Others, thinking more kindly toward him and his politics, said he was only protecting the queen's property."

"Did anyone ever find it, the queen's property I mean?"

Auntie's pale blue eyes caught Amy's. "You've been talking to those Winters children, haven't you? They're a meddlesome pair. You mind what I told you. It's family that counts."

"But this is family. Philo Coburn is family."

"He is that." Auntie paused for a moment, still looking at Amy, then went on. "Philo Coburn was an honorable man. He'd have had nothing to do with any royalist trappings left by Seth Howes. He did his duty toward the dead man—buried him right and proper and paid for the stone, too. No one owed him anything more."

"But he was their rector, their neighbor. What about Lucy? She must have known him."

"Of course she knew him. And she'd have had no more to do with him than her father did. Loyal patriots they were, the lot of them." She reached out and took Amy's arm. "I've stood in the hot sun long enough. Take me back to your grandmother's table."

They moved slowly from the family grave site to the far side of the church, where the booths and tables were set up. People smiled and nodded as they passed, but Auntie's grip on Amy's arm never slackened, nor did she pause to acknowledge the greetings. It embarrassed Amy to be led by this old, ill-tempered woman through the festive crowd without a sideways glance. With considerable relief she delivered Auntie to her chair at Grandma's table.

"Back at last, and high time it is," Grandma said. "You know what the doctor said, Matilda. You're not to stay on your feet too long. And look at you. Out walking and standing for an hour in the hot sun."

"I've little enough time left for it, Louise. That hour is nothing in the face of eternal rest. Now don't go fussing over me." Auntie waved her cane in Grandma's general direction. "And you, child, stop your fidgeting."

Amy was shifting from one foot to the other, impatient to be away, to be a part of the crowd circulating around the church. The hushed, respectfully lowered voices of visitors to the churchyard had given way to clear laughter and chatter at the Fair tables, and Amy was eager to share in it.

"Of course she's fidgety," Grandma said to Auntie, giving Amy a hug. "You would be, too, if you were fourteen and had spent the entire morning with two old women in church and then in the cemetery! And on such a beautiful day!"

For the first time Amy noticed how beautiful a day it was. "Real New England weather," she recalled her father exclaiming on those rare days in Maryland when the humidity was low and the temperature moderate. But those were poor imitations of this day. Everything sparkled in the cool, bright sunlight, which deepened the blues and greens of the shade while it bleached out the colors in the open areas. The crystalline quality of the air gave every sound a pleasant, bell-like tone, which complemented the hues of the fading summer and the colonial costumes of the parishioners. The sky was so blue, the day so clear, that every leaf on the trees was distinct. Amy inhaled deeply, filling her lungs with the fresh, clean air, shaking off the disturbing events of the morning. As though she had just awakened to the activities of the day, she noticed that things were happening around her. Already the main road was filled with Sunday drivers, people who had come to visit the Fair as well as tourists and antique dealers from more distant, larger cities. Suddenly Amy wanted to be among them, to belong to St. George's Fair, to be one of those whose picture was indulgently snapped by city folk as an example of rural charm. On the far side of the church driveway a long table had been set up and loaded with platters of fried chicken and tubs of corn on the cob. The smells drifted across the lawn, enticing people to line up for lunch. Not only did Amy want to be involved in the bustle of activity around her, she also realized that she was hungry, ravenously hungry. "Isn't it time for lunch?" she asked.

Grandma laughed. "I'm sure it must be. There, I see Betsy's just finished her tour, she's waving you over. Why don't you go on with her and picnic?" She reached in her apron pocket and took out a worn leather change purse. Extracting a dollar bill, she handed it to Amy. "Here, this should be enough for whatever you want. Go on with you now."

Released, Amy spun on her heel and ran across the driveway to the church steps where Betsy was standing. Just now she wanted to hear no more warnings from Auntie about Betsy and Ben, nor to delve any further into the family history that so obsessed her great-aunt. Even her shyness at joining the group of young people with Betsy could not hold her back. She was drawn to them as she was to the food and to the holiday atmosphere of the day, to the business of the present. Skipping up the church steps, Amy felt the shadows of the past slip from her. She became, like Betsy and her friends, an actor in a memorial pageant rather than a participant.

After the initial awkwardness of the introductions had passed, Amy began to relax. The contrast of Amy's softly Southern accent with the clipped Yankee speech led to an exchange of colloquialisms that soon had the entire group giggling comfortably.

"I can't wait to tell my mother I'm going to 'ret up' my room," Betsy said in her best imitation of Amy's Maryland expression. "She'll never guess I mean clean it up. She'll probably tell me it doesn't need any more wrecking."

"And wait until my mother asks me if I've finished retting up mine," Amy added, "and I answer, 'Aaayuh, my room's clean.' I'll never hear the end of that!"

"But you have an advantage over us," one of the other girls said. "Wasn't your father raised here? He probably talks just like us."

"I guess I never noticed it," Amy said. "I never thought much about his being from another part of the country."

Her own words were an unexpected reminder of where her parents were at that moment, far away in another part of the country. That distance seemed suddenly unbridgeable, an awesome gap in time and space. A hard, painful knot swelled in Amy's chest, overwhelming her joy in the day and in her new friends, eliminating her hunger. The surge of homesickness, that intense desire for the familiar, swept away every sensation except the raw ache of being alone. For an instant Amy thought she was going to cry. Her throat tightened, and her eyes burned with tears. But Betsy, glancing sympathetically at her, launched into a vivid impersonation of how a Yankee turned Southerner turned Midwesterner would sound.

"After your dad's lived out there for a month," Betsy concluded, "it'll take him half an hour to say squirrel. He'll sound like he's got a mouthful of r's when he talks." She demonstrated, making them all laugh. Amy joined in, thinking what a special person Betsy was. She was like a trim little bird, a cardinal, her hair and eyes the same muted shade of reddish brown as the female of that species. And like the bird, Betsy paid quick and complete attention to whatever caught her eye, applying a cool, level-headed appraisal to the events around her. Just being with Betsy eased Amy's sense of displacement and put her world back into its familiar perspective.

"Thanks, Betsy," she said quietly as they all walked over to the lunch table. "Talking about my parents like that made me realize how much I miss them. If you hadn't made me laugh, I don't know what I'd have done. I feel like such a baby, but I can't help it. You must think I'm really stupid."

"Are you kidding? If my parents left me alone with relatives I barely knew, I'd make so much fuss they'd probably never come back for me. Oh, I'm sorry." Betsy clapped a small hand over her mouth. "What a dumb thing to say!"

"It's all right. I did feel abandoned, out of place, as though I didn't quite fit here. At the same time—" Amy paused, then shrugged off the thought. "I don't know. At the same time I feel as though I've been here before. Maybe it's being around Grandma again after all these years."

"And maybe it's pure and simple hunger. You're probably hallucinating. Let's eat."

As they moved down the line, Betsy introduced Amy to the women serving the food—the rector's wife, Betsy's mother, the choir leader and church organist, and a woman named Hat McFee. The faces were different and the names, but Amy recognized them as the working women of the church, the ones in every parish who make the potluck suppers and the covered-dish dinners a success. The New England winters had reddened their hands and cheeks to a deeper hue, and their chins seemed sharper, their lips thinner, than those of the women at the parish in Maryland. Yet they were just as ready to give an extra dollop of potatoes or a better-than-average slice of pie to their young, hungry clientele. Perhaps things were not so different here after all.

"Thank you, ma'am," Amy said, receiving her loaded plate from the tall, angular woman at the end of the table.

"You can call me Hat. They all do. You're young Paul Enfield's girl, aren't you?" When Amy nodded, the woman clucked her tongue softly behind her teeth. "Skinny, just like he was, and can probably eat your way through a side of beef and be ready for a sandwich when you're done. You tell your grandma she's got no more excuse not to come to tea. You can sit with your aunt for an afternoon. You tell her Hat's expecting her."

"People around here sure do have funny names," Amy said when they were all seated under the big sycamore tree on the church lawn. "Hat McFee? Is it short for Hattie? And what's Hattie short for?"

"That's not really her name," Betsy replied, laughing. "She's called Hat because she leaves a man's hat hanging on the porch outside her front door, a felt hat in the winter and a straw hat in the summer, so it looks like there's a man in the house. Only there isn't."

Amy giggled. "That's like hanging a 'Beware of Dog' sign in your window when you don't own a dog. Does it work?"

"It must. She's never had any trouble."

"But neither has anybody else," another of the girls commented. At that they all began to giggle, sitting together with their plates of chicken and corn balanced on their knees, the calico prints of their long skirts moving brightly in the soft, warm breeze. For the first time since she'd been told she was coming to live in Grandma's house, Amy felt a deep grin stretch over her face, a grin that sprang from a sense of well-being, from a sense of belonging once more, at least for the moment, in a particular spot in time and space.

VII

Lucy Griffin

Night came suddenly to the old house on Constitution Hill. The autumn twilight hung briefly over the ridge as the sun dropped, lengthening the shadow of the house down across the meadow until it swallowed up the elm in the front yard. And then it was dark; the peak of the hills cut off the last of the sun's light. From her window Amy could see lights turning on in the valley and a twinkling of headlights as cars moved along the highway below. There was a pale glow from the church steeple and occasional flashes of light from the parking lot as the clean-up committee finished its chores and went home. The Fair had begun closing down in late afternoon, after the handmade quilts were all auctioned off and the home-baked pies were sold, and Grandma had no more preserves left on her table. Amy had nearly fallen asleep in the Winterses' wagon, watching the regular nod of the mules' heads as they plodded up the hill to the farm. After a light supper of soup and sandwiches, she had come up to her room. Ostensibly she was writing a letter to her parents; instead, she sat at the window, watching the night fall.

Her father had sat in this same house as a boy, looking out over the soft hills. Somehow his presence lingered in the shadowed nooks and corners, a warm and comforting reality. Amy had no physical image of him as a child, beyond the sepia-colored likenesses of old photographs in the family album, and the sense of his having lived here, of having left something of himself, was more real by far than those. It brought her parents closer, made writing to them unnecessary. Besides, she could not describe in words her feelings about the old house, about Auntie and Grandma, and not to do so seemed a lie of omission. She sat on her bed, one hand curved around the bed-post, thinking instead of writing.

She wondered whether Grandma, and Auntie before her, had sat and felt the smooth, carved surface of the spindle bed, and whether they, like Amy, enjoyed the feel of the repeated pattern beneath their fingers. Standing up, she followed the design all the way to the top of the post, where it ended in the acornlike knob. The wood was dark and smooth with the polish of generations of hands and furniture oil. To Amy it was irresistible, demanding to be touched. Holding the knob, she swung gently around, back to her seat on the bed. The acorn turned beneath her hand. Startled, thinking that she had broken it off, Amy jumped up and inspected it. The knob was firm in the post. Curious, she tried turning it again. With a squeal of dried wood, it began to unscrew. Carefully she re-moved it. The grooves were neither chipped nor worn, but the bottom of the acorn had been whittled out perhaps a quarter of an inch. Standing on tiptoe, Amy peered into the hole at the top of the bedpost.

"Why, it's hollow." Reaching up, she felt into the hole with her forefinger and touched a soft, cottony mass. Stretching both her forefinger and middle finger into the hollow, she caught and pulled out the soft material.

"At least it wasn't a spider's nest!" She squeezed the cloth in her hand. "There's something inside it."

Quickly she pulled away the material. There on the palm of her hand was a tiny gold key, no more than half an inch long, wrapped years ago in the now disintegrated piece of muslin.

"A key! But a key to what?" Amy glanced around the room looking for a jewel box, a desk drawer, something small enough for the tiny key to fit. But the top of the bureau was clean, covered only by the embroidered strip of linen. Her night table was also bare. Before she could consider further, there was a soft tap at the door. Unwilling to share her discovery or reveal its hiding place, Amy tucked the key back in the muslin and pushed it down into the hollow. Quickly she screwed the acorn back on the bedpost.

"Amy?" Her grandmother stepped into the room. "You weren't asleep, were you?"

"No, ma'am. I'm just sitting here," Amy replied, relieved that Grandma had not seen the antique poster bed with its knob removed.

"I hope you aren't trying to write in the dark." She switched on the lamp, and Amy blinked at the sudden light. "I've brought some cocoa and cookies. It's been a while since dinner." She set a tray down on Amy's desk and looked at her granddaughter. "And I thought you might be lonely."

The tears Amy had held back that afternoon burst unexpectedly in hot, wet splashes down her cheeks. "It isn't that I don't like it here," she said in a quavering voice, brushing at her eyes with both hands. "I don't know what's the matter with me."

Grandma sat down on the bed and pulled Amy close to her. "I know," she said, patting Amy's head gently and rocking her slightly. "It's a big change."

"I guess I'm just tired."

"As well you should be. But part of it is the time of day.

The shadows always seem to me to bring back the past, memories I thought I'd filed away for good. Why, after your grandfather died, I cried every night—and I had your father for company. I guess we all resent time; it changes us, and we can never go back."

She said it so sadly that Amy pulled away from the damp spot she had left on Grandma's shoulder. "Did he die in a war, too? Auntie says this family is always waiting for wars to end."

"Auntie says a lot of things about the past. But no, your grandfather survived his wars. He died of tuberculosis. That's why we came back here, for the clean air. He was living in the city when I met him, working to save enough money to go to college. He'd have been the first in his family to get a real education. I guess it was too much for him, working and studying and trying to support me, and then your father. By the time we came back to the farm it was too late." She paused, then straightened up and cupped Amy's face in her warm hands. "He'd have been so proud of you and your father. It's selfish of me, I guess, but I'm glad that you had to come to stay with us. Shall we have our cocoa?"

"Does Auntie feel the way we do, about memories and the past?" Amy sat cross-legged on her bed, sipping the cocoa.

"Perhaps more than we do. Her world is always in shadow, after all. She has little but the past to think about."

"What was she like before, when she could still see?"

"She was very nearly a grown woman when I was born, Amy. After she married Plyn, she lived in the wing of the house and helped my father run the farm. Johnny and I used to drive her wild; she was a hard worker, and we were two mischievous children." Grandma shook her head and smiled down into the whirlpool of cocoa she stirred up with her spoon. "I used to think she was mean to break up our games and make us do the chores. It wasn't until I had a child of my own that I realized it wasn't meanness, just a powerful belief in discipline. She and Plyn never had any children, so Johnny and I got the brunt of her child-rearing ideas."

"Did she ever do anything ... unusual?"

"She made the best hot cakes east of the Mississippi." Grandma looked up. "But that isn't what you mean, is it?"

"I'm not sure what I mean. She's different from anyone I ever met. And Betsy says she can see things other people can't."

"Now, don't you go believing all you hear. Matilda uses her other senses to make up for her lack of sight. She notices almost everything, which surprises people, even mystifies them. They tend to exaggerate her abilities. But being blind, or almost, doesn't cripple your mind or your feelings. As for seeing things, let's just say Auntie remembers well. When she was a child there was no radio. Families sat around the fire and read aloud, or told stories. She knows all there is to know about this family, and about most of the people in the village, because she remembers."

"But it's as though she really knew them. She talks about Lucy Griffin and Philo Coburn, even Seth Howes, as if she had met them and lived in this town with them. Did she tell you their stories?"

"I'm afraid I rarely sat still long enough." Grandma smiled again. "I was a great disappointment to her, I think. As a child I was too headstrong, too impatient to listen. To me it was just history. And I was selfish. I wanted to be out having fun, skating on the lake, visiting my friends. Poor Johnny covered for me many a time, doing double chores so I wouldn't be punished. I often felt that Auntie was waiting for something, that she expected something of me, but I was too busy enjoying myself to worry much about it. And then when I was fourteen. . . ." She hesitated and looked up at Amy. "Now just listen to me. You're tired and I'm talking the night away at you. Unlike me at your age, Amy, you are a good listener."

"It's all right. I'm not sleepy. Please go on. What happened when you were fourteen?"

"My brother Johnny died," Grandma said quietly. "It was such a stupid waste, a freak accident the doctor said. He'd had a tooth pulled and somehow got blood poisoning. We were all. . . ." She waved a plump hand as if to brush away the memory. "We were all distraught. I couldn't stand it here without him. My mother had a friend in the city, a dressmaker. She sent me there to live, to learn dressmaking. I hated it, having to sit still all day and sew. But Madam was kind; she liked me, partly I'm sure, because my hands never perspired and I could work on the fine laces and silks without damaging them. And then I met your grandfather." She finished her cocoa and set the cup back on the tray. "And the rest you know."

"What about Auntie? When you came back here, was she still waiting?"

"She was still here, of course. But she had changed. Or I had. Now that I had a family, I wanted to know more about our past. I guess I had grown up. She told me whatever I wanted to know, the facts of births and deaths, but it was as though she had lost interest in it all. Then, as she aged and grew more dependent on me, we became closer. I learned that there was something she had lost, something she thought that as a child I could help her find."

"The legacy?"

"You certainly are a good listener." Grandma glanced at Amy from under raised eyebrows. "Yes, Auntie calls it that, but I've never really understood what she means."

"It has to do with Lucy Griffin, though, and this room, doesn't it?"

"That I can't tell you, dear. You'll have to ask Auntie." Grandma got up, took Amy's cup, and tucked her into the quilt-covered bed. "It's time we both got some sleep. Don't forget, you start school tomorrow." She pulled the covers up around Amy's chin and kissed her gently on the cheek. "Good night, dear."

Amy lay in the darkness, the cocoa warm inside her, trying to sort out the events of the day. The sudden, total change in her surroundings was disorienting. Against this new setting the realities of home blurred, as though the first fourteen years of her life were set aside, complete, and irrevocably consigned to the rapidly fading past. She had been at the farm less than forty-eight hours, yet it seemed much longer; the explosion of knowledge of her family's history had flung her backward in time, linking her with the homestead and its people. Her parents seemed very far away, but the familiar sting of home-sickness was gone.

She slept deeply at first, lost in the cottony night quiet. Hours passed, and slowly the rhythms of her rest changed, her eyes flickered behind closed lids, and Amy began to dream.

She stood barefooted in the room, on the smooth but rough-hewn floorboards. With that peculiar logic of dreams, she knew it was night although the room was illuminated. It was rather like looking into a silver globe in the garden of some grand estate, seeing the lines of the house distorted and reduced. The walls curved outward around a glow of light like a great bubble. Within it was the spindle bed, the table and chest of drawers, the braided rug on the floor, and standing by the window, a slim, tense shape. Slowly the figure turned, and Amy recognized the girl in the portrait.

Lucy Griffin, a small book clasped in one hand and a velvet pouch swinging from the other, stared past Amy. Her lips moved in a hollow whisper.

"Father?"

Amy glanced behind her, but the doorway was a black abyss, silent and empty.

Lucy waited, then laid the book on the table next to her bed. For a long moment she stood looking at the room as though she were memorizing the shape and placement of each familiar object. Gently she touched the quilted coverlet, the contoured post of the spindle bed, the smooth wood tabletop. Then, with a deep breath, she turned and thrust open the window. Without a backward glance she gathered up her skirts and, still clutching the velvet pouch, she prepared to step out onto the porch roof.

With the opening of the window the focus of Amy's dream shifted. A strong wind, neither warm nor cold, batted around her, pressing down on her legs, her back, her hands. The window itself seemed to widen to take in the meadow below, with Lucy poised in the foreground at the window ledge. The field tilted down in a shimmer of starlight, visible, yet closed in night, its long slope interrupted only by the shape of a small sapling where the great elm now stood in the front yard. Far below Amy could see the steeple of the stone church. The landscape was vacant of roads and houses, of clusters of trees, all erased by the reeling back of time. Suddenly a figure appeared, cloaked in black, running from the far side of the meadow toward the house. Lucy saw him and waved, motioning him back to the shadowed contours of the meadow. But the figure came on, dodging across the field, never looking up. Lucy glanced behind her, then waved more frantically.

"Seth," she called. "Seth, wait. Go back!"

Her voice wavered, a thin ribbon of sound above the house

and yard. And then a shot split the still night and echoed across the darkness. Lucy sat frozen at the window, the running halted in mid-step. A second shot sounded, and Lucy's hands gripped whitely on the window frame as she leaned forward, her mouth wide in her pale, small face.

"No, Seth! No!" she cried, and the wind blew the words back to Amy as the dark figure in the field stumbled, staggered backward, and fell.

"Father?" Lucy pushed herself away from the window, catching her skirts on the sill, and ran across the room toward the doorway and stairs. No longer a black space, it widened before her, and her voice floated back to Amy. "Father, what have you done? It was Seth, Seth. . . ."

The voice trailed off, the room darkened, and Amy felt the rough floorboards give way to cool smoothness of sheets. She was lying again in the snug spindle bed, the quilt heavy over her. A queer, thin song rose around her, wordless at first, then more clearly. "How's her name . . . the key . . . L . . . M. . . ."

As though in response to its rhythms, Amy's legs and body were prodded and pushed in time with the chant. The weight of the quilt insulated her from the touch of the small hands that patted gently but insistently, shaking her out of the depths of the dream. At the very edge of sleep, Amy sensed an urgency in the persistent buffeting. There was something to be done. She willed her eyes to open, to peer into the dream darkness and see the person whose invisible hands demanded that she wake. But her lids were heavy as the quilt and unresponsive. She lay, unable to move, as the prodding hands, less gentle now, shook the bed. The chant increased in volume, surrounding her with waves of hollow sound.

"How's her name . . . the key . . . L . . . M. . . ."

Amy sat bolt upright, suddenly wide awake. Moonlight filled the room with a soft, colorless sheen. It was absolutely quiet, yet the chant hung in Amy's mind. The bedclothes were twisted around her legs, and her skin retained the sensation of the weight that had moved over her in sleep. She stared at the closed door of her room, half expecting Lucy to appear in front of it. Caught in the vividness of her dream, she waited, hands clenched, staring into the still room. Nothing had changed, no shadows moved, no wisp of curtain stirred in the night breezes. But the acorn was gone from the spindle bedpost. Glancing down, Amy saw she held the knob in her left hand, and in her right, warm against her palm, lay the tiny gold key.

"'L . . . M . . . the key,'" she repeated the chant. It continued to beat in her mind, and the key tingled hotly in her hand. "A key, but a key to what? Tell me," she demanded of the empty, still room. "What do you want?"

Her voice cracked the weight of silence, breaking through the relentless chant. It receded like a wave on a distant shore, and the key quite suddenly cooled. The room, still moonlit, now filled with night sounds—the breeze rustled the elm outside her window, birds twittered the coming of dawn. Amy pulled the quilt aside and jumped out of bed. The elm stood huge and firm in the front yard, the road was clear below, etching its way among trees and houses into the valley.

"It was only a dream," she whispered to herself, "from listening to all those stories Betsy and Grandma told me." She looked again at the key in her hand, then out over the meadow. The spot where Seth Howes had fallen was hidden by the elm, but Amy could visualize it, as much a witness to his death as the house and the tree itself had been.

She picked up the acorn knob, felt on the bed for the piece of muslin, and rewrapped the key. She had no memory of removing it from its hiding place, no sense of the texture of the wood in her hand, no awareness of the key at all, until she awoke and felt the metal hot against her palm. Slowly she put it back in the hollow of the bedpost and screwed the knob firmly in place. For a long time she stood with her hand on the wood, as Lucy Griffin had done, recalling images from her dream. If she could remember clearly enough, perhaps the connection between them and the insistently repeated chant would become obvious. But whatever it was escaped her, something barely seen and noted only in the unreachable depths of her subconscious. Finally she climbed back into bed and lay thinking, watching the early morning light fill the room.

VIII
School

Amy's dream so preoccupied her that she did not think of her first day at school until Grandma called her to get up. Then the magnitude of starting a new school alone, of entering classrooms filled with strangers, overwhelmed her and replaced all other concerns. Wishing she had consulted Betsy about what to wear, she changed her clothes three times before selecting her best pleated wool skirt and the pale green sweater that accented her hazel eyes. By the time she got to the kitchen for breakfast her hands were cold with nervousness. Somehow she swallowed the hot oatmeal Grandma prepared and listened to the directions for getting the school bus. Amy was relieved to hear that Ben and Betsy also took the bus and would help her to find her way to classes.

"You don't have to worry about a thing," Grandma said, helping Amy on with her jacket. "Those Winters children will take good care of you."

"I thought you didn't like them."

"If I didn't like them I wouldn't bother to scold them. They remind me of myself and Johnny—too full of life for their own good sometimes. But a little mischief never hurt anyone." Grandma gave Amy a quick hug and handed her a brown paper bag. "Here's your lunch. You can buy milk at the cafeteria. Run along now, so you don't miss the bus."

Amy started out the door, then turned back. "Grandma, would you mind if I invited Betsy to come home with me after school? If it wouldn't upset Auntie?"

"Don't you worry about Auntie. This is your home, too, now, and high time it had some young people laughing in it. By all means bring Betsy home, and anyone else you'd like to invite."

Now all I have to do is to convince Betsy that it's safe to come over, Amy thought as she ran down Bridge Street toward the bus stop. Betsy's hesitation about being around Auntie was understandable; Amy's own reluctance to be with the peculiar old woman was akin to fear. But if they were to solve the mystery of the silver they would need Auntie's knowledge of the past.

At the bottom of the hill Amy stopped and looked back. In the clear, blue-edged morning the house appeared very different from her first impression of it. The sun was shining full on the front porch, highlighting the fading green of the elm and brightening even the worn white clapboard shingles. With its windows open to the fresh autumn air, the blinds pulled up to take in the maximum of sunlight, the old house seemed a warm and inviting place. Amy smiled up at it and then, impulsively, waved before crossing the street to the bus stop.

She had been waiting only a few minutes when the yellow bus came around the curve and stopped for her. Hers was one of the first pickups so there was a selection of seats. Clambering up the bus steps, Amy nodded to the other passengers and slipped quickly into the first unoccupied seat she came to. Although she thought she recognized some of the faces from the church Fair, Amy felt shy about talking to any of these young people. They might not remember meeting her, or might remember and not want her company. She perched by the window, waiting to be spoken to, to be invited to join them. For a few minutes after she got on, the bus was unusually quiet, the churning and grinding of the old motor drowning out the subdued whispers and giggles. But very soon the early morning chatter resumed its normal level, ignoring and excluding Amy. She stared out the window, concentrating on spotting Ben and Betsy at each successive stop, and on trying not to look too eager for attention, or too proud to accept it.

As the bus neared the town, the stops became more frequent and the rolling hills of pasture and crops gave way to lawns and driveways. Like smooth, green welcome mats the trim front lawns stretched back from the road beneath tall, shade-thick trees—elms, maples, oaks, and sycamores. The houses faced the street in white dignity, the New England salt-box style with its clapboard siding and shutters and deeply slanted rear roof, set off by an occasional Greek revival type with columns around the front porch and two lateral wings, or by a turreted Victorian mansion. The overall impression of the town was one of tidy green peace and quiet. No papers blew in the gutters, no hedges grew ungainly and untrimmed, no lawns showed the unsightly browning of drought. The great trees seemed to shed serenity from their arching boughs as gently as they did the frequent summer showers on the grass, the rooftops, the brightly colored beds of perennial flowers.

Approaching the center of town the road split, branching around a park labeled the town commons by a small sign that also identified the tiny log cabin on its western edge as the oldest building in the town. Facing each other across the commons were the post office and the library, each housed in the white frame, black-shuttered structure so characteristic of the area. And at the far end of the commons, at the top of a small rise, was a white Congregational church with a tall, pointed steeple. Amy looked eagerly from one side of the street to the other as the school bus bounded along its route, but the scenery went by too fast for her to take it all in. She caught a glimpse of shops down a side street, an ice cream sign, and a movie marquee, all tantalizing in their unexplored newness. And then the town was behind them. Reaching the end of its circuit, the bus swung back on the main highway, traveled another three or four blocks, and stopped in front of a white picket fence where Ben and Betsy were waiting.

As soon as the door opened, Ben leaped up the steps and swung into the aisle next to Amy's seat. His dark red hair was still wet from its morning brushing, but already it was out of control and hanging in his eyes. Although he was dressed neatly in denims, a plaid shirt, and pullover sweater, the clothes hung on his lanky frame like afterthoughts, necessities that were hardly worth his attention. In fact, Ben looked as though he considered morning itself not worth his attention, a time of day redeemed only by the possibility of breakfast. Still, he radiated energy and carried into the bus with him a rush of fresh air and the clean scent of toothpaste. Amy smiled up at him, relieved to see a friendly face at last.

"Good morning," he said, stumbling as the bus started up. "Nice of you to save a seat for me. I didn't know you cared."

"But I don't," Amy stammered, blushing. "I mean, I didn't save the seat for you." She glanced over her shoulder, wondering if the entire busload of students was listening to them.

"She was saving it for me," Betsy said, pushing Ben aside and sliding into the seat. She glared at her brother, who grinned and loped off unevenly to the back of the bus. "Don't mind him," she said to Amy. "He's just teasing."

Betsy settled down, smoothing her skirt and rearranging

her notebooks on her lap. In total contrast to Ben, she was calmly and neatly organized, completely unruffled. "Can you believe anyone can look that bad that fast? He's incredible," she added, shaking her head. "By the way, thanks for saving me the seat. Usually we have to stand."

"It wasn't difficult."

"Most days the bus is full by the third stop," Betsy began, then glanced sharply at Amy. "But you don't know anyone. I keep forgetting. And no one even said hello, much less sat down, right? They certainly know how to make a person feel at home! Are you nervous?"

"I really am. My hands are like two ice cubes."

"Don't worry. It's a small school. By this afternoon you'll know everyone. They probably already know you."

"They do?"

"It's a small school in a small town," Betsy repeated. "And for some reason Ben's sort of important around here. Don't ask me why. Every girl in his class will want to know how you got him to notice you."

Again Amy felt her face redden, and yet she was glad she had worn her special green sweater. Betsy paid no attention to her embarrassment as she busily prepared Amy's orientation to the school by drawing a map.

"The office is here," she said, marking it with an X. "I suppose they have your records. They'll give you a schedule and I'll show you where the classrooms are. The day will be over before you know it. And here we are."

The bus stopped in front of an ungainly red brick building. Two sets of heavy wooden doors topped a wide, fan-shaped set of stairs, bounded on each side by a sweeping stone banister. Students gathered there in clumps, standing or leaning against the warm stone, absorbing the sunshine until the last possible moment. The building had two stories, with wings to the right and left of the entrance. Three sets of three windows marked the rooms on each level of both wings—high, wide windows that could be opened and closed only with long wooden poles. The shades were uniformly drawn halfway down, giving the building a sleepy but unblinking expression. White stone framed the main doors and the windows, and there was a sculpted white stone cornice around the roof. Above the doorway was a crest of white marble beneath which was carved, "District Regional High School." Trying not to appear nervous, Amy followed Betsy through the gathering of students, up the front steps of the building and inside, down the hall to the office.

Once Amy's schedule had been established, Betsy helped her find her locker and then guided her to her first class and introduced her to her teacher. Amy settled quickly into the classroom routine of homework assignments and seating charts. Now that she was officially established as a newcomer, the students were friendly and helpful. She got from class to class without getting lost and was relieved to find that she was on a par with the other students in her subjects. Even the building itself, with its familiar school smells of chalk and floor wax and pencil shavings, and its desk tops carved with the initials of long-graduated students, helped to set Amy at ease. When the final bell rang, she joined her classmates in gathering books and jackets from lockers, shyly talking with them as they all left the building.

"Do you think you could come over this afternoon?" Amy asked Betsy as they waited for the bus. "There's so much I want to ask you about, about the school and the town and all. And something I want to show you," she added quietly.

Betsy's bright brown eyes met Amy's. "You didn't find it, the silver?"

"Nothing like that," Amy answered, "but I think I have a

clue. Something strange happened last night." She paused as their bus pulled up and opened its door. Together she and Betsy were jostled aboard and tumbled into a seat. "It's going to sound a little crazy," she added when they were settled.

Betsy leaned forward eagerly. "Go on. Tell me."

Amy hesitated. To Auntie, strangers were a threat to the family legacy. To tell Betsy and Ben anything was a betrayal of her past. And if Betsy didn't believe her, she'd be humiliated. But they had agreed to work together. She took a deep breath and began to relate her experience.

"Maybe you better not tell Ben," she said when she had finished. "If he didn't believe me about the man in the church, he'll never believe I didn't make all this up."

"But you have the key. I mean, that's a fact. If we can figure out what it opens or even why it was hidden, Ben will have to listen."

"That's one of the reasons I want you to come over. You might notice something that I missed."

Betsy frowned, thinking. "You actually dreamed what happened? You saw Lucy Griffin and Seth Howes? And Lucy woke you up?"

"Something woke me up. But it wasn't like a dream, Betsy. It was more like watching a play."

"You don't have to be wakened from a play. It must have been a dream. Maybe it means that you know something you don't know you know. And that's why you dreamed about it. But we can't count on it as the truth."

Betsy was right, of course. Dreams were not reality. It was silly to take the events of a dream so seriously—if it was a dream. And it must have been, created by her own subconscious. Still, the memory was so vivid to Amy that she could not dismiss it as an image of her own invention.

"Was either one of them carrying anything?" Betsy asked.

"Not that it would help much. We wouldn't know what they did with the silver even if they had it with them that night."

"The only thing was a book. Lucy was carrying a book when I first saw her, and a velvet sack, a sort of purse."

"That's no good. You can't hide silver in a book or in a purse."

"It might have been big enough," Amy said, considering. "And you could write down in the book where it was hidden. I wonder if Auntie knows anything about it. We could ask her."

"She won't say anything, not with me around. You know how she feels about Ben and me."

"We can try. But please, let's not tell Ben just yet."

"Don't tell Ben what? That you're still seeing ghosts?"

Both girls swiveled around. Ben was leaning over the back of the seat, his chin resting on his folded hands.

"It's too late not to tell Ben," he said. "I heard the whole thing. Not that I care about your dreams. Unless you already know where the silver is, your dreams won't do us any good."

Amy glared at him. "This isn't just a treasure hunt," she snapped. "That house has secrets, Lucy Griffin's secrets, and I mean to find them out. Maybe you don't care about anything but the silver, but I do." The image of Lucy's face when Seth fell in the meadow flashed through Amy's mind. "I care about those people, and I ... I want to help them."

She turned away from Ben and Betsy and stared out the far window of the bus, embarrassed, unsure of what she meant. The night before the house had been heavy with the pain of those old secrets, secrets Amy was determined to unveil. While Auntie's pale, blind eyes saw inward, back to the roots of the family, Amy had had only a glimpse of its history and she had to have more. She had to understand the curious effect the house and its occupants had had upon her. With or without Ben and Betsy she would unlock the past. And she could begin by concentrating on the reality of the key. A key had a lock, and a lock had something of value behind it. The legacy, the silver —it no longer mattered what she found, only that Amy satisfy her burgeoning curiosity about her own history. Ben was tapping her on the shoulder.

"Look," he said. "I'm the one who should be angry. We're supposed to be working together, and the first thing you do is tell Betsy secrets. Some partners you are."

"Look who's talking," Betsy answered. "If you won't believe anything Amy does tell you, why should she tell you anything?"

"Just because you two are dying to believe in ghosts"— Ben snickered at his pun—"doesn't mean I have to be. But, all right. I'll help your ancestors if you'll help me find the silver. Are we partners or not?"

"We're partners," Amy said after a moment. "But we've got to trust each other."

"It's a deal. You handle the ghosts, and I'll take care of the silver." After agreeing to tell Mrs. Winters where Betsy had gone, Ben slipped out of his seat and into the aisle, rejoining his friends at the back of the bus.

"Brothers," Betsy snapped as he left. "You should be glad you're an only child."

IX

Aunt Matilda

"You're sure your grandmother said it was all right for me to come?" Betsy asked as they walked slowly up Bridge Street. "I wouldn't want her getting mad at me again."

"She thinks the house needs some livening up. It's been a long time between generations. And she wasn't really angry with you."

"But your aunt was. If I get sent home in disgrace again my parents will kill me."

"Don't worry. Grandma's really nice, and Auntie's just a bit peculiar. She has this thing about the family. But if she realizes we're interested in the old days . . . and you are, aren't you, Betsy? It isn't just the silver, is it?"

"I'd like to find it, if that's what you mean." Betsy stopped in the road, balanced on one foot, and shook a stone out of her shoe. Then she looked up at Amy. "What about you? Don't you care about finding it?"

"I don't know. That chant last night, the words on Lucy's gravestone, the key—they're clues to something, something more than the silver. Until I came here I never thought much about my family, about what kind of people they were or where and how they lived. But now I just have to find out, or there'll be something missing in me. I can't explain it."

They continued up the hill and around to the back of the house. Amy pulled open the scraping screen door. The kitchen was empty and cool after the bright fall sunlight, and the house itself was quiet.

"Come on upstairs," Amy said. "Auntie and Grandma must be resting. I'll show you the key."

They tiptoed up the stairs and into Amy's room, shutting the door quietly behind them. Amy set her books down on the table and unscrewed the acorn knob from its post. Carefully she removed the muslin and unwrapped the key into Betsy's hand. Betsy held it, turning it over on her palm, then looked around the room.

"It's awfully small. There's nothing here it would fit. Besides, nothing here is locked up." She closed her hand around the tiny key and waited, then handed it back to Amy. "Does it feel warm, the way it did last night?"

Amy shook her head. "No. It wasn't just warm, it tingled. And I don't hear anything either. Last night it was all connected, the chant, the key, the dream. Can't you think of anything it might fit?"

"A jewel box maybe. Or, I know, a diary. You know the ones with a clasp?" She frowned. "But it could be anyone's diary, not necessarily Lucy's. What's that?"

The tap of a cane sounded in the hallway. Quickly Amy thrust the key back into the bedpost and screwed the acorn in place. The tapping stopped outside her room.

"Lucy? Lucy, is that you?" There was a pause, then Auntie opened the door. She stood erect in the doorway, holding her cane, then reached in her pocket and put on her glasses. Her face was flushed, and her eyes gleamed behind the thick lenses.

"It's Amy, Auntie. I've brought Betsy home with me."

The flush faded as the old woman turned toward Amy's voice. "What are you doing here?" she asked.

"We just got home from school. We tried not to disturb you. Grandma said it was all right."

"Grandma?" A spark lit the tired eyes for a moment longer, then died. Auntie sagged heavily onto the cane as though the weight of her years had fallen again on her frail shoulders. When she spoke, her voice sounded old and cracked. "Grandma. Of course. But I don't like it, child," she said. "You've no need to let strangers poke about here. You've other, older friends to meet."

"And I will. But Betsy's really interested in the past, in the house and its history. That's why I asked her over. We want to learn about it. Won't you help us, Auntie? You're the only one who remembers." Amy tried to meet the old woman's gaze, but Auntie seemed to be looking beyond her, focusing on some distant point of time and memory.

"I know Philo Coburn built the house, and Lucy Griffin was born here." The words tumbled out, as though Amy could weave with them a net to catch and hold her great-aunt's attention, to bind her to the present. "But what about the others? Please tell us."

Ignoring Amy, Auntie turned toward Betsy. "You, Betsy Winters," she said, pointing a bony finger at the girl, "what concern of yours are the Griffins? You and your brother came snooping around the house. What did you want? Why didn't you just come to the door and ask?"

"We didn't want to disturb you," Betsy stammered. "I'd been reading about the church, for the Fair, and this house is of the same period. The old rectory is gone. Ben and I thought we'd just look around."

"Don't lie to me, young lady." The gnarled finger waggled under Betsy's nose. "You were looking for something. Tell me what it was and why, or you'll not spend another minute in this house."

"Yes, ma'am." Betsy backed away from the old woman, moving closer to Amy. "You see, we read about Seth Howes...."

"Seth Howes was a traitor. He was not welcome in this house."

"But he took the silver," Betsy went on over Auntie's interruption. "He took it from the church and he had to leave it somewhere. We thought it might be hidden here."

"You thought this family would harbor such a man?" Auntie stepped forward, brandishing the cane less at Betsy than at the memory of those old hostilities.

"No, Auntie." Amy shoved Betsy behind her. "They might not even have known. The more we learn about that time, the easier it will be to solve the disappearance of the silver. That's why we need your help."

There was a silence in the room for a full minute. Amy and Betsy stood still, impaled on Auntie's glinting, impenetrable gaze. At last she spoke.

"That's all you wanted? The silver?"

Betsy nodded. "Yes, ma'am."

"And you, child. Is that what you want?"

"I'd like to find it, but more than that, I want to know about that time, about the people. They're my family."

Tapping her cane, Auntie walked across the room to the window overlooking the meadow. "I won't have you interfering," she said to Betsy. "If you and your brother try to make this a treasure hunt, as though we were a family of pirates, I'll chase you out as fast as I did before. But if you want to learn, you're welcome in this house."

"That is what we want," Amy said. "Honestly, Auntie, you won't be sorry. Tell us first about Lucy Griffin."

Auntie continued to look out the window. "This was Lucy's room. She lived all but one year of her life here, sleeping in this bed, sitting at that table. It was her room even after she died; my grandfather, her son, locked the door and left it for twenty-two years, until I was born. It was my room until I married, and now it's yours, child."

"Was she here the night Seth Howes was killed? Or was she married by then?"

"She was here. Good Christian that she was, she tried to save that wretch's life. But Philo Coburn was a good shot. Seth Howes died. Lucy blamed her father. The war was over. A senseless death, she called it."

Auntie spoke slowly, as though she were reciting a nearly forgotten passage from her own youth. When she paused, Amy asked a question.

"Was Lucy expecting him that night?"

"Was she expecting Seth Howes to come here?" Auntie turned away from the window and looked at Amy. "Of course not," she said in her normal tone. "They had welcomed that man to this town, built his church, and supported him. He confirmed the children of this village and then preached them loyalty to the king. Is it any wonder the people drove him out? When Seth Howes took the British side, Philo Coburn forbade his family to set foot in the church, or to speak to him."

"Maybe Lucy did anyway."

Auntie's back stiffened, her chin went up. "Philo Coburn was a patriot. He lost two sons in that war, Lucy's brothers. Seth Howes betrayed the cause they died for. Do you think she'd have gone against her father's wishes after that?"

"It just seems so sad, to lose a friend that way."

"He was no true friend, child. His allegiance was to King George, not to the Americans."

"Still, it seems a shame that her father killed him."

"Politics killed him, Lucy said. Within a month she'd married the widower Griffin and moved out of her father's house."

"But she came back."

Auntie nodded. "You've a good memory, child. Yes, she came back. Griffin's sons resented her and the son she bore their father. When the old man died, they denied her a place in his home, at his table. So she made her peace with Philo Coburn and came back to the farm to raise her son. And a hard life it was, too."

"She never married again?"

"She hadn't much chance, between raising the boy and tending the farm. I remember how she looked. . . ." Auntie cleared her throat, and her blank, unseeing eyes swept over the two girls as though recording the expressions she could not physically see. "That is, I remember my grandfather telling me how she looked with the mule's reins draped around her neck, plowing the fields in her father's old boots. She worked like a man to keep this place."

"You know so much about her," Betsy said. "Did she leave letters, a diary, something we could look at to get to know her better?"

"She left her family," Auntie said, raising her cane to point to Amy. "Her children and her children's children, and the portrait, of course. You must show Betsy the portrait, child. If she is to learn the history of this house, she should meet its mistress. Come, help me downstairs. I'm ready for my tea."

"And high time, too." Grandma stood in the doorway. "I thought I heard voices. But, Matilda, you mustn't tire yourself like this with all those stories."

"The child wants to learn, Louise. She's not too young to understand death and honor."

"Death and honor will have to wait until after tea. Go on,

girls, go look at the portrait while I take Auntie downstairs. It's time she rested."

Betsy and Amy ran down the stairs to the living room. The portrait was in shadow, untouched by the sun in the rear, western windows. Lucy Griffin's pale face gleamed in the dim light.

"She does look like you," Betsy said. She looked from the painting to Amy and back again. "Except for the color of the eyes." Suddenly she grinned. "I've got a great idea. We always have a Halloween party at the church. Why don't you dress up like Lucy Griffin, and the rest of us can dress like other founders of the town. Do you think we could come here for part of the party? I'd love to see Ben's face when he sees you next to the portrait."

Auntie and Grandma had stopped in the doorway of the living room. "Lucy Griffin, come home again," Auntie murmured. "You're an observant child, Betsy Winters. Perhaps it would be a good idea to gather the colonists in this room once more."

"I think it would be delightful," Grandma said when they were all seated at the kitchen table with tea and biscuits. She thought a minute and smiled. "Do you remember, Matilda, the parties we had here when I was their age? There were all sorts of games on Halloween, even a treasure hunt. The house was full of people then, and dancing. I'll talk to Father John. I'm sure we can arrange it."

"We always bobbed for apples," Auntie said. "It was the one time I could get you and Johnny into the orchard to pick instead of just climbing the trees. The big tub is probably still in the barn, Louise. We could use that and some of the Northern Spies. But I suppose our tree doesn't bear fruit any longer."

"We'll get the apples, Auntie." Amy reached out and

touched her hand, looking up into the thin face. At that moment Auntie smiled, and a faint blush of color tinged her cheeks. Amy squeezed her hand and suddenly laughed out loud. "We'll climb the trees, won't we, Betsy, and fill barrels of apples. It will be just the way it was when you were young. We can pop corn in the fireplace and tell ghost stories. Oh, it will be a grand party."

"And a fortuneteller, we'll need a fortuneteller," Grandma said. Her eyes sparkled and she chuckled. "I told a pretty mean fortune in my day, didn't I, Matilda? Why, I once told Emma Gould she was going on a trip, and she fell off the back porch that very night on her way home."

Betsy began to giggle, and Grandma's chuckle expanded, joining Amy in deep draughts of laughter, until even Auntie's shoulders shook with a thin, rasping cough of mirth. The kitchen filled with sound that crackled against the old walls and windows, absorbing the years of silence. Finally Grandma sighed and wiped her eyes.

"Oh, my dear children," she gasped. "What a joy it is to have you here. But from the look of the shadows, Betsy, it's time you were leaving. Amy can walk you partway home."

"Thank you very much for letting me come, Mrs. Enfield. I'll show Amy the shortcut so she'll know how to get to my house. It's nowhere near as far as it seems on the bus," she said to Amy. Then she touched Auntie's shoulder. "And thank you, too. I'm sorry Ben and I upset you."

"No matter now, Betsy."

"Off with you, now," Grandma said, shooing them into their jackets, "before it's dark. You see that Amy finds the right path back."

X
Déjà Vu

The shadows of late afternoon cut deeply from the hills down across the meadow. Amy and Betsy set off on the faint path that led diagonally across the hill toward the church, talking about school, their assignments, the teachers, and the people Amy had met. At the edge of the meadow, Amy stopped to zip up her jacket against the sudden chill of the autumn evening and looked back at the farm. The lights from the kitchen were blocked off by the side wing, and the house brooded in stiff silence.

"It certainly isn't a very happy house, is it?" Amy commented. "At least not from this angle. Just think of all the people who have lived and died there—my grandfather, Aunt Matilda's mother and father and husband. . . ."

"Not to mention your friend Lucy." Betsy shivered, pulling her own jacket close around her shoulders. "The way your aunt talks about her is enough to give me the creeps. It's as though she knew her."

"Maybe she did." Amy stood still, looking back at the house where a touch of white fluttered at the living room window. "Grandma must have left the window open," she said absently. "I'd better close it when I get back. Auntie'll get a chill."

"It gave me a chill when she called you Lucy upstairs in your room. But you were right," Betsy added quickly, "she's nice once you get talking to her. Do you suppose she knows anything about the silver?"

"I don't know." Amy turned slowly away from the house and walked beside Betsy down the path. "Somehow I think she'd have told you if she did, just to get you and Ben out of the house. At least we know that Seth Howes saw Lucy that night, the night he died, so what I saw could be the truth."

"What you dreamed, you mean. I wish we'd asked her about the key."

"You think she'd have left it in the bedpost if she knew about it?"

"Maybe she wanted you to find it."

"Or maybe she didn't. I'd hardly be likely to go around unscrewing bedposts on my second night there. Next time you come over, let's search the attic. We've got to find what that key opens. What's that? Do you hear someone?"

Betsy listened for a moment, then laughed. "It's the brook. It does sound like voices, doesn't it. Remember, I told you this is where Ben and I were when we saw the barn. The water's just ahead through the trees."

She led Amy into a thick grove of old birches, glistening white beneath their dry, browning leaves. The branches arched gracefully into the air, casting a mantle of stillness over the twilight, broken only by the sound of the running water. Amy hesitated, looking up into the darkening sky, and reached out to run her hand along a smooth, black-penciled trunk.

"Have you ever swung birches, Betsy? Climbed up the very top, until the tree begins to bend under you, and tossed out your feet and ridden it to the ground?"

"I don't like it. The ride's okay, but it's buggy, and I

always get scratched coming down. Ben swings them all the time." She turned to look curiously at Amy. "Are there birches in Maryland?"

"Of course there are, but. . . ." Amy's fingers tingled at the touch of the white bark, and closing her eyes, she could almost see the delicate, wavering balance of the treetop, smell in memory the bitter green of crushed leaves as the tree bowed toward the earth under the climber's weight, crashing upward again when set free. "But I never did it." She looked ahead through the gathering dusk. "And yet I remember it, as though I'd watched someone swing these birches when they were saplings. I remember it all—the brook with the flat white stone, the waterfall, and now these birches, except that they were smaller."

"Your parents probably brought you here for a picnic when you were a baby. Or maybe your father told you about the birches. You said he used to fish here."

"I suppose so. It's just so familiar. I feel it." She let go of the tree trunk and rubbed her hands together hard to rid them of the prickling sensation.

"Cut it out, Amy. Next you'll be telling me that you know where my house is without having been there."

"No." Amy frowned, puzzling over this glimpse of a memory that was not really her own. It shifted in and out of her mind like sunlight in deep water, never quite illuminating the depths. It was irritatingly illusive, and the more she concentrated on it, the less clear it became. "No, it was before your house, before any of these houses. And these trees were small, more like bushes. She was barefooted, running through the rows of corn with her skirts hiked up, just the way I thought she'd be, laughing, with her braids unpinned."

"Who was running? What are you talking about?"

Amy blinked. "Lucy, Lucy Griffin. I could see her just now, running toward this grove."

"Now? Coming here?" Betsy whirled around, looking over her shoulder. But the meadow was completely shadowed by the hills, and only the white columns of the birches were clearly visible in the soft light. "Let's get out of here!"

"I don't really see her," Amy said, catching Betsy's sleeve. "Only in my mind."

"Just the same, I've got goose bumps all over. Besides, it's late. I've got to get home. Come on."

Betsy trotted ahead through the grove and bounded across the brook on the series of flat stepping stones with Amy close behind her. The water of the brook quickened as it flowed past the flat white stone, and invisible above it the small waterfall tumbled into a deep pool. The crust of dried lichen on the rocks crumbled under their feet as they crossed, rasping harshly above the fluid bubbling of the water. Betsy reached the far side and veered to the right to pick up the path down the hill. It was wider here, and well traveled, cutting through banks of wild raspberries. The girls were running now through an open field. Below them Amy could see the dark silhouette of the elm that marked Seth Howes's grave and the sharp point of the steeple of his church. Finally Betsy stopped, breathless, at a fork in the path.

"The one on the right leads down to our house," she said. "See where the picket fence is? If you go straight on, you'll come to the village. It's quite a hike, but you can get there. Can you find your way home all right? It's nearly dark."

"I'll be fine. See you tomorrow?"

"Sure. On the bus." Betsy started down the hill toward her house, but after a few steps she stopped and turned back. "Amy, remember at the church when you thought Ben and I were trying to scare you?"

"Yes, but that was only because of what Auntie said about you, and finding Seth's grave and all. I don't think that anymore."

"No, I know that." Betsy scuffed a small rock out of the path and kicked it to one side. "What I mean is, you aren't just making this up, those visions and stuff, just to impress me or something? We could be friends anyway, without Lucy Griffin." She looked up again, solemn faced and serious.

Amy hesitated. Maybe it would be better to tell Betsy that this was all a joke, a gimmick to help get acquainted and make friends in her new home. Better to be accused of a white lie than to have Betsy think she was crazy, or at best, peculiar. Being separated from her parents, moving in with Grandma, and meeting the strange and forbidding Aunt Matilda had been disconcerting enough without the inexplicable events of the past few days. To alienate Betsy would be to cut herself off from people her own age, to isolate herself in the Griffin household. And she could understand Betsy's not wanting to be made a fool of. Yet she could not bring herself to deny this past which so insistently forced itself upon her. The images were faint even now, coming to her fogged by years and weakened by generations. To lie to Betsy, she felt instinctively, would blur them further, perhaps obliterate them entirely.

"I'm not making them up," she said at last. "Maybe I'm imagining things, but I haven't deliberately invented anything I've told you. If that makes me odd, someone you'd rather not be around, I'll understand. But I wouldn't do it on purpose, honestly I wouldn't."

Betsy listened, her head cocked to one side, until Amy had finished. Then she nodded once, sharply.

"Thanks. I believe you."

"And we're still friends?"

"Of course." She grinned suddenly, her small face bright in the dim light. "How many friends can I have who see ghosts? I'll ask my mother if I can come Saturday to check out the attic."

"And bring Ben," Amy called as Betsy ran off down the hill. "He can help us move the heavy stuff."

Amy made her way back along the path, hurrying as the twilight deepened. The raspberry bushes were dark clumps on either side as she approached the stream, their jagged leaves catching at her skirt. Nearing the water, she heard again the rushing of the brook. It struck and splashed on the rocks, silvering them with spray that caught the last light of the day. Picking her way across the stream, Amy smiled, thinking how like a young woman's laughter the voice of the brook was. The image of Lucy racing through the cornfield toward the water came to her mind again.

It's a place she would have liked to come to, Amy thought, pausing on the far side of the stream. While Auntie spoke of Lucy Griffin as a hard-working, rather somber figure, Amy saw the face in the portrait. That girl would have had a secret place, a haven to retreat to when the chores were finished, or even before they were finished, her braids flying, coming undone. "I wonder how long her hair was," Amy murmured, touching her own brown braids. "I'll bet she hated to have the snarls combed out as much as I do."

Amy stood there, reluctant to leave this peaceful spot, though the light had dimmed sharply when the sun dropped below the hills. The birch grove was still and motionless, the birds already nested for the night. Amplified by the ceiling of arched branches, the sound of the brook was pure and clear.

"Lucy?"

Amy glanced sharply upstream.

"Lucy." The voice was full, resonant as the deepest currents of the stream. "Lucy, you were such a happy child."

"And you have made me a happy woman." This second voice was higher pitched, but sweet in tone.

Amy squinted into the shadowed reaches of the upper brook. Two figures stood facing each other on the flat white rock, their hands clasped together. Faint as they were, Amy recognized the young Lucy, her brown hair loosed in ripples down her back. The dress she wore was of a light color and seemed to shine against the dark coat and trousers of the man with her. His hair was silvery blond, and the features of his face were cruelly etched by the shadows.

"It is no happiness to be torn from your family, wrenched from those good people onto an island of hate."

"Not of hate, Seth, but of love. Their passions cannot touch us, no more than my father can reach out from his land to this rock on which we stand. Our house is firmly built, as the good Scripture says, and their anger flows past us as the water of this brook washes around the stones that bound it."

"My weakness has changed your life, not for the better I fear."

"Is it ever weakness to admit love? When you preach love, do you preach weakness?"

"I have taught you too well." He smiled and touched her cheek gently with his large, bony hand. "You argue for faith more convincingly than I."

"Never that. It is you who led me, you from whom I've learned my faith."

"Yet you were barely able to sit still long enough to memorize your catechism. What a beautiful child you were, Lucy, so full of life and joy."

"Because I was with you those hours. I loved you even then."

"Hush, lest you blaspheme. You were too young to love."

"Too young to be taken seriously. I loved you then, and I love you now, and I shall love you for all eternity."

"Then I am blessed. But Lucy," he reprimanded gently, "by the law a woman must be modest in all things."

"My words are but a modest statement of my humor, good priest," she said, dropping her eyes virtuously. "Surely you would not have me lie."

He drew her to him, with a hearty laugh that echoed on the ripples of the brook. But in a moment he was serious again. "You have no regrets then, my Lucy? You may still return that which I have entrusted to you. Nor is it too late to repudiate your vows."

"Is your resolve so pale that you ask your freedom?" She pressed away from him, looking up into his eyes.

"Indeed not, my dearest. My heart is yours, to hold and keep while man shall walk this earth, and past the Day of Judgment, if so the Son of Man shall rule. But with it I give you only hardship and pain. If you have any doubt, the faintest hesitation, tell me now. I know not what the life I offer you will hold for us."

"You need not know. Know only that I have accepted it, and that I will keep your trust till you see fit to redeem it."

They remained there, their hands clasped as before, looking into one another's eyes. The brook swelled and ran around the flat white rock, musical as ever, yet somehow muted, as though it were muffled by distance. Amy stood among the birches, back from the bank, watching, aware only of the two people on the rock.

"Amy? Aaaaa-meee!"

She started, looking over her shoulder through the birches to the house. Walking rapidly across the meadow, her white apron a bright patch in the evening, came Grandma. Quickly Amy looked back to the brook and the flat white stone. It lay as before in the middle of the stream, but Seth and Lucy were gone.

"I'm here, Grandma," she called, her breath coming out in a rush, as though she had been holding it for some time. With a last glance at the brook, she turned back to the path and ran out through the birches into the meadow.

"I've been calling and calling," Grandma scolded when they met. "I thought surely you'd gotten lost up here. Why, it's pitch dark. Didn't you hear me? What on earth took you so long?"

"I'm sorry, Grandma. I guess Betsy and I just got to talking, and I had to find the path on the way back."

"It was your first day of school. And girls will chatter, I suppose. But don't make a habit of frightening me like that," she scolded with a smile. "And look at you, out here in all this dampness with only that light jacket on. You'll catch your death of cold. Whatever will your parents think if I let you get sick? Come quickly now. Supper's ready and then some."

Shooing Amy ahead of her, Grandma marched back along the path through the deep, damp meadow grass. Once inside the house, Amy turned to go into the living room.

"Come along now, Amy. Wash up and sit down. Dinner's on the table."

"Yes, ma'am. I just want to shut that front window. I noticed that you'd left it open."

"Not that window, dear." Grandma glanced into the living room. "That hasn't been opened in ten years, I'd wager, not since Plyn's death. The sash is broken, and I've never gotten around to having it repaired. The house is cool enough in summer with the elm to shade it."

"But I saw the curtain blowing," Amy began to say. But was it the curtain? Or the pale flutter of Lucy's muslin dress as she ran through the twilight to meet Seth Howes on the flat white stone in the center of the brook?

XI

The Attic

"The middle of October and look at it," Grandma said, slamming down the window above the sink where she and Amy were doing the breakfast dishes. "It might as well be the middle of November, it's miserable enough. I don't suppose Mrs. Winters will be letting the children out in this rain, Saturday or no Saturday."

"Couldn't you call her, Grandma? They couldn't come last week, or the week before, and we've been planning this for ages. Either Ben has a football game, or we've got too much homework, or there's something on at the church. Today's the perfect day. Please?"

"You certainly have been busy," Grandma agreed, smiling. "I'm glad you've settled in so quickly."

"There's just so much to do!" Amy exclaimed. "Everybody's been talking about the Halloween party, too. Betsy thought we might find some good costumes in the attic. It isn't really cold out, Grandma, just rainy. Ben and Betsy must have slickers and boots. Besides, we'll be dry enough in the attic."

"Don't know why children love an attic so. There's nothing up there but dust and the excess baggage of five generations of Griffins."

"We just want to look around." Amy wiped the dishtowel damply around a mixing bowl. "You said it needed cleaning up."

"That it does. But don't think you're going to drag all kinds of junk from up there down here. There're more than enough knickknacks around this house now to keep me busy dusting till doomsday." She dumped the dishwater and wiped her hands on her apron. "I suppose it wouldn't hurt to call. Perhaps Mr. Winters could pick them up this evening if the weather gets worse."

"Oh, thank you, Grandma." Amy hugged the round figure, pressing her face close to the soft, rosy cheek. It was something she did not understand, how Grandma could be so soft and squeezable, like a velveteen doll, when Auntie, who had the same father at least, was so bony and unapproachable. She dried the silverware, polishing it till it shone, listening to Grandma's half of the conversation with Mrs. Winters.

"Can they come?" she asked when her grandmother hung up.

"If they don't, Mrs. Winters won't survive the day." Grandma was laughing. "Betsy's been nagging her about it all week. She says to expect them in about an hour, which gives you just enough time to get your chores done. Take Auntie's tea up to her and make your bed. By then it will be time to punch down the bread."

Amy tapped lightly on the door of Auntie's room before she entered. "Good morning," she said, setting the tea tray on the table beside the bed. "Did I wake you?"

"I haven't slept, child. I sometimes think that God in his wisdom denies rest to the aged because he knows that soon enough we will rest for eternity. Help me up, child. The dampness of November is in my old bones this morning."

Amy slid her arm beneath the old woman's shoulders and lifted. Even through Auntie's thick flannel nightgown she could feel the small, brittle bones, the fragility of the aging body. Auntie was almost weightless, as a sparrow fledgling blown from its nest is too light to be held in the smallest child's hands. Supporting Auntie with one arm, Amy propped up the pillows for her to lean back upon. Perhaps it was her nearness to the end of life that made her so remote from human touch; to envelop her in the gentlest hug would be to chance crushing to dust the worn but stubborn frame. Wrapped in the past, she was insulated from the emotions of the present. Gently Amy smoothed the quilt over her lap.

"Would you like your tea now? I'll pour it for you. Grandma's bringing your breakfast in a minute." Amy leaned over and whispered, "And it's real food this morning. We made pancakes, doctor's orders or not."

"With real maple syrup, I hope." Auntie's face creased unexpectedly into a smile. "I'll try to act surprised. Open the blinds, child. I might as well see the rain while I suffer from it."

"I like it," Amy said, pulling back the drapes and looking out over the damp gray meadow. "I mean, since it doesn't give me aches and pains, I sort of enjoy a good rainy day. It's perfect for exploring the attic."

"The attic, is it? And what do you expect to find up there?"

"Probably nothing. But we'd like to look at all the old things anyway. There must be trunks full of stuff up there."

" 'We'?"

Amy turned away from the window and looked at Auntie. "Betsy and Ben are coming over. But they won't be any trouble, honestly, Auntie."

"As long as they don't interfere, child."

"Interfere with what, Auntie?"

The pale, veiled eyes swung toward the window where Amy was silhouetted against the rain-splattered glass. "You don't know yet? When is your birthday, child?"

"My birthday? In December, December twenty-sixth. Why?"

"We've very little time left, then, even less than I thought." She pushed up against the pillows, raising herself higher and speaking in a clear, strong tone. "You must pay attention. There are things in this house for you to notice, and you must be ready to receive them. The next time may be too late, certainly too late for me."

"What next time?" Amy ran over to the bed and knelt down beside it. "Auntie, you must tell me what you mean. I want to help, but it's all so confusing. Please . . . ."

But the old woman dropped back onto her pillows, the tea cup and saucer rattling on her lap. "Hush now, your grandmother's coming."

"But surely she knows?"

"Hush, child!"

"Keeping Auntie company are you, Amy, while she has her tea?" Grandma bustled into the room with a steaming, covered plate, carrying with it the rich smells of fried bacon and golden brown pancakes. She removed Auntie's tea cup and helped her sit up straighter on the pillows, then set the breakfast tray down and swept off the cover with a flourish. "A real treat this morning, Matilda. Not as good as yours used to be, though I used your recipe, but hot cakes just the same. Now, get along with you, Amy, and get your chores done before your friends arrive."

"Remember what I said, child. They mustn't interfere."

"Nor you either, Matilda. We can't keep Amy cooped up with us two old crones. She needs her young friends. I'll see they don't disturb you."

"If it's all right," Amy said to both of them, pausing in the doorway, "we'll come and visit with Auntie later, after we've finished our exploring. We've still a lot to learn about this house."

"After this breakfast, I ought to be equal to you three youngsters."

Grandma looked from one to the other, sensing a change, a softening in the old woman's attitude, and an eagerness in Amy's. But she said only, "Don't overtire yourself, Matilda."

Wrapped in one of Grandma's huge white aprons, Amy was punching down the bread dough when Betsy and Ben pounded on the back door.

"Come in," she shouted, rubbing the sticky dough off her hands. They burst through the door, rivulets of water running from their hats down off their slickers into puddles on the kitchen floor. "You're soaked," Amy said, wiping her hands and helping them with their slickers.

"People who go out in the rain usually do get wet." Ben scowled at her. "Or hadn't you noticed? It was quite a trip just to poke around in a dumb attic."

"Stop complaining," Betsy said, jabbing a small fist into her brother's shoulder. "You don't seem to have shrunk any from getting wet. You're just afraid of a little hard work."

"I'm not afraid of anything," Ben snapped, and flicked a spray of cold rain in Betsy's face. "I'm here, aren't I? Let's get at it."

"It ought to be a lot of fun, with you being so cheerful and all," Amy remarked and got her own cold splash from Ben in response. He grinned, his usual good humor restored. He and Betsy mopped up the wet floor and hung their dripping coats in the pantry while Amy finished the bread and covered it with a clean linen cloth. She set it to rise again on the shelf above the radiator, removed her apron, and turned to Betsy and Ben.

"Ready? Let's go."

They clattered up the stairs and down the long hall past Amy's room to the attic door.

"Won't we need a flashlight or something?" Ben asked. "It's pretty dim outside today."

Amy switched on the light. "It is an old house, but we do manage to have a few modern conveniences."

"I mean for back in the corners," Ben said, hesitating as the girls started up the stairs. "We don't want to miss anything."

Glancing at the single bulb that hung from its cord in the center of the room, Amy nodded. "I guess you're right. There's a flashlight on the shelf in the pantry, by the back door."

"I'll get it." Ben disappeared down the steps into the hallway.

At first glance the attic was a disappointment. The room ran the length of the original portion of the house. It was floored, with a window at each end. As Grandma had said, it was a catchall for the castaway goods of the Griffin family. Disassembled baby cribs and bedsteads leaned against the rafters, side by side with sprung armchairs and three-legged, uncaned table chairs. There were carefully labeled cartons of baby clothes and dishes, a wheel-less carriage and wigless dolls. But nothing seemed to be much older than Amy herself, as though the present generation had choked out the remnants of an earlier time. Betsy and Amy were surveying the jumble in silence when Ben returned. He flashed his light into the dark recesses of the eaves, causing long fingers of shadow to leap about the room like black, heatless flames. Above them the children could hear the heavy beat of the rain and the sweep of the elm's branches as the wind blew through it.

"Don't, Ben." Betsy shivered as the light danced over the shrouded, lumpy shapes that filled the attic. "It gives me the creeps, as though all those things are alive. There sure is a lot of stuff."

"It's a good thing you did bring me along," Ben said and set the flashlight down with its beam directed under the dark slope of the roof. "We'll have to move all this to get to the interesting part."

"What interesting part? I don't see anything."

"Logic, Amy. If you were storing junk, you wouldn't put it behind what was already here. You'd just keep putting things one in front of the other until you ran out of space. Looks to me like we have to start in the twentieth century and work our way back."

Amy nodded. "Of course. And Grandma did say she wanted things cleaned out. We can make three piles—the keep, the throw out, and the who knows? When we're finished Grandma can decide what she wants done with each."

"Then we'll have to inspect all the boxes, too. That alone will take us a week. We'll never get done," Betsy moaned.

"Not really." Amy grunted, pulling to one side a carton marked dishes. "For now we'll only look through the ones packed before 1840. That's about the time Lucy died. The quicker we sort this stuff, the quicker we'll get to the old trunks."

The stacks Amy had designated grew rapidly as the children pulled out the familiar items from their own time— a toaster without a cord; a dome-shaped radio, its speaker broken; a box of drapes and window curtains, worn and sun-rotted. Ben found the first treasure, leaping onto it with a whoop. It was an old rocking horse, its tail reduced to a few strands of hair, but its stirrups and bridle were still intact. Ben rocked out of the corner toward the girls, fanning the horse's flanks, his long legs bent on each side of the rockers.

"Say, don't you wish you'd had this as a kid? Whose do you suppose it was, Amy? Didn't your dad ever mention it?"

"Not that I can remember." Amy stroked the paint-chipped nose of the horse. "We'll have to ask Grandma. With a little work he could be beautiful again. Put him in the keep pile for sure."

Ben slid the horse to the corner by the stairs where the girls had piled some old record albums and an incomplete set of Horatio Alger books. Slowly a path was forming down the center of the attic as the children pushed and shoved odd boxes and broken furniture into piles near the steps. By noon they had worked their way midway across the attic. Their hands and faces were gray with dirt and smudged with the cobwebs that caught and stuck on their hair and clothes. After moving an ornate Victorian mirror from Amy's side of the attic to a place next to the rocking horse, Ben wiped his hands on his overalls and sat down on the red painted saddle.

"What do you say we take a break and see what your grandmother's got for lunch," he suggested. "In this dust I'm not sure I'd recognize a clue if I fell over one."

"Wait, Ben." Amy peered up at him from behind a shrouded horsehair sofa. "I've found an old trunk back here. Bring the flashlight. Maybe we are getting closer."

She disappeared again as Ben and Betsy stumbled through the piles of boxes to the sofa. The trunk was tucked far under the rafters, its rounded top covered with dust and strapped by two leather belts. The leather split and crumbled as Amy worked the buckles free. Gently she pulled on the lid, which fell back unevenly on its aged hinges.

"It's old, that's for sure," Betsy said, as Ben aimed the flashlight into the trunk. "Look at that lace."

Amy brushed her hands off on her shirt, then lifted the folds of material and shook them out. "It looks like a wedding dress," she said, holding the yellowed material in front of her. "I wonder whose it was."

"Try it on, Amy, please. It's so beautiful."

"It will never fit me, Betsy. I'm way too tall. You try it. But you better wash up first," she added, noticing Betsy's grimy hands and face. Ben bent back over the trunk, poking down toward the bottom.

"There's nothing in here but clothes," he said in disgust. "And I suppose you two will want to play dress-up for the rest of the day."

"It'll only take a minute. Besides, you were the one who wanted a break." Betsy climbed out from behind the sofa and ran down the stairs. "I'll be right back."

Ben continued to dig in the trunk while Amy took the dress into the cleared center of the attic, looking for a place to hang it. The yellowed satin gleamed in the dim light, as if it held still the soft warmth of candles from times gone by. Here beneath the old beams of the house, in the attic, rain-darkened and smelling of age and camphor, it was easy to imagine the past peopled with the wearers of dresses like the one she held. She turned and said, half to herself and half to Ben, "You don't suppose it could have been Lucy's, do you?"

Ben stood up, swathed in a black wool cloak. "No more than this could have been your Philo Coburn's. It's a little moth-eaten, but not ancient. Like the effect?"

He stepped out from behind the sofa and stood in front of the mirror by the steps, swinging the cape on his arm, Dracula fashion. "All I need now is a sword. . . ."

Amy looked up as he stopped abruptly. He was staring into the mirror, his face pale and rippled in the old glass. Suddenly he swung around, dropping the cape beside him on the floor, and stared beyond her into the far end of the attic.

"It isn't you," he said in a choked whisper. "You're standing up. The mirror and the dress...."

Before Amy could respond, he had kicked the cape aside and was running down the stairs two steps at a time, his shoes banging heavily on the bare wood. Slowly, the hair prickling at the base of her neck, Amy turned, backing toward the stairs as she looked where Ben had been staring. A pale figure sat by the far window, her hand on the weathered sill. She stood up and beckoned to Amy.

"I did not betray him," she said. "You must tell him."

"Lucy?" Amy's voice sounded hollow in the empty attic, as though the discarded stuff of the years beyond Lucy Griffin could no longer muffle it. The figure moved closer, and Amy recognized the face from the portrait. But Lucy looked older, her eyes large and deeply shadowed, her mouth no longer smiling.

"I meant only to protect him, to see his memory rightly honored. You must seek him out. The answers lie with him."

Her voice was soft, a sigh among the rushes of rain and wind. Amy stood still, a great wave of pity replacing her original fright.

"Tell me what to do," she whispered. "I'll help you."

Sadly Lucy shook her head. "He was lost to me through anger, and in anger I swore my revenge. I held his trust in love, and lost for bitterness eternal rest. Seek him out. Return Seth Howes to his church and my trust will be fulfilled."

"But how? How can I give his church back to him? Tell me what to do."

The figure seemed to waver, as lights flicker in an electrical storm, but remained standing a few feet from Amy. "Listen to what I say. What love hid must come to light again in love."

She turned full face toward Amy, and the lines of her

mouth softened into the near smile of the portrait. For that moment her features were clear, her voice still low but strong.

"Return him to his church, I pray you," she repeated, "else I am not freed from my word. I have sworn to see him honored in his church once more, before its legacy shall be restored. The end of life releases us not from our vows. The legacy must be restored before I come to rest."

"The legacy? The silver and the legacy are the same?"

"Seek the outward, the visible sign, that we may be blessed with inward grace. The legacy is in his name. . . ." Lucy's voice faded and her face blurred once more in sadness. She reached out one hand to Amy, clinging a moment longer to the foreign century. When she spoke again her words were but intermittently audible, her form thinner, receding into the past.

"Life . . . denied . . . mourning . . . . Only an open heart . . . see truth . . . Seth . . . the key . . . seek L . . . M . . . ."

She was gone.

XII

Second Sight

"Wait," Amy cried. "Don't go!"

"I just came back." Betsy paused at the head of the stairs. "What's the matter? Where's Ben?"

"Downstairs I think, if I'm not too late. Here." Amy thrust the dress into Betsy's hands as she ran past her. "Try it on if you want."

Ben was in the pantry with his slicker on, staring at his rain hat. He turned toward Amy when she stopped in the doorway. Amy wondered whether her own eyes were as wide and startled as his. His lips were thin and bloodless, barely moving when he spoke.

"I'm leaving," he said.

"You saw her, too. She was really there."

"Something was there." Ben lifted his hat off the hook and held it crumpled in his two hands. He hunched his shoulders beneath the slicker as though trying to shake off the crawling chill on his neck. "Whatever it was, I can live without it. And if you had any sense, you wouldn't get involved either. Unless you can't help it." He looked curiously at her, his eyes narrowing. "It only happens when you're around."

For a moment Amy stared blankly at him, not comprehending. But as her eyes recorded his suspicious regard of her, his stiff posture, his recoil as she neared him, an icy understanding crystallized within her. Like the people of Salem who blamed their troubles on the supposed witches in their midst, Ben thought she was responsible for Lucy Griffin's appearance. He'd transferred his fear of the apparition to her, as though she possessed an eerie and possibly evil magic.

"It isn't me," she protested. "You saw her, too. It's Lucy Griffin and she needs our help, that's all. I talked with her."

"You said you talked to Seth Howes, too." Ben looked down, concentrating on his hat. "I don't believe in ghosts."

"But you did see her."

"It could have been an illusion, something about the mirror. And that guy in the church must have been one of the parishioners."

"You saw him, too!" Amy remembered suddenly Ben's odd behavior in the church that first Sunday morning, his denial of any knowledge of Seth Howes. She looked at Ben as though she were seeing him for the first time. Like masks that fright had snatched away, Ben's teasing smile and deliberately rumpled appearance were gone, and she could see how much like Betsy he was. "Why didn't you tell me?" she asked softly.

Ben shrugged. "I figured it had to be someone playing a joke on us. It was different from . . . from this. He was standing there in the vestibule when I came in. She just appeared. One minute there was only my reflection in the mirror, the next minute there was hers, watching us." He shivered.

"But there's no reason to run away from what happened." Amy reached out and touched Ben's arm. He did not pull away. "I was scared, too, you know. But they don't mean any harm."

Ben continued to twist the hat in his hands. Finally he looked directly at her. His eyes were troubled, serious, but the shock and suspicion were gone. "Nothing like this ever happened around here, at least not to me, before you came. Maybe it's some kind of a trick you play."

"And maybe it happens all the time, but people are afraid to talk about it, to share it."

He glanced down again. "I just don't like it. Hunting up old treasure was one thing. Stirring up ghosts is another."

"I don't think we've stirred them up," Amy said slowly. "I think they've always been here, waiting for someone to see them, to talk to them."

"I don't want to see them. Or talk to them." Ben jammed the hat on his head, his face closing behind a frown.

"But Ben, we can help them." It was suddenly terribly important that Ben stay, not because he was Betsy's brother, not because he was a partner in the search for the silver, but because he was Ben and shared with Amy the sensitivity that allowed them both to experience the presence of Lucy Griffin and Seth Howes.

Roughly Ben turned away from her. At the door he stopped, his hand on the latch, and looked back. Their eyes met, acknowledging for an instant the bond between them. Then Ben pushed the hat back on his head in the old, casual way.

"What about the silver?" he asked, clearing his throat. "Did she say anything about it?"

"Not exactly. It's like a riddle I've got to figure out, but there are too many things I don't understand."

"You're not making this up, are you, about talking to them." It was a statement of fact, as though Ben had just discovered the reality of magic and had no more need to catch the magician up in his sleight of hand. "What did she say?"

"Lots of things that don't make sense, like having to give Seth Howes his church back."

"We can't exactly invite him to give the sermon on Sunday," Ben mused. "She didn't tell you anything useful?"

"She can't, I guess. She said she promised, that she gave her word and can't break it. But it's all mixed up with this house and the church and Auntie, and something about love finding what love hid."

"What's love got to do with it?"

"I'm not sure." Lucy's words were jumbled in Amy's mind like pieces of a jigsaw puzzle in a box, unrelated now, but able to be fitted together into a logical pattern. And suddenly two pieces meshed. "Suppose we aren't the only ones, Ben. Suppose someone else has seen her."

"Like who?"

"Like the one person who knows more about the history of this house and village than anyone else. Betsy said the towns-folk think Auntie's got second sight, that she sees things. We can ask her."

Ben hesitated, remembering his last encounter with Amy's great-aunt. But his fear of things inexplicable, as well as his dread of the old woman's anger, rapidly took second place to his desire to find the silver and help Amy solve her mystery. He pulled the hat from his head, jammed it back on the hook, and unsnapped his slicker. "I suppose it can't hurt," he said and followed Amy through the dining room and into the front hall. Betsy was just coming down the stairs. She was wearing the yellowed wedding dress, and her brown shoes and heavy wool socks stuck out incongruously below it.

"You might have told me you weren't coming back," she said, planting herself in front of them. Hands on hips, jaw clamped in annoyance, she glared at them. "What's going on?"

"It's Lucy Griffin," Amy started to explain. "When you went down to wash your hands Ben saw her in the mirror."

"You saw her?" Betsy sat down abruptly on the steps. "She was there, in the attic?"

"Ask Amy. She talked to her."

"What did she say?" Betsy glanced from one to the other, her eyes round and questioning. Suddenly her eyebrows shot up under the fringe of brown hair that fell over her forehead. "And you left me up there alone?"

"She'd gone by then," Amy said. "I could barely hear her at the end, like trying to understand a radio station through static."

"Just the same, you might have warned me. Weren't you scared?"

"We were both scared," Amy admitted with a sideways grin at Ben. "But then I just felt sorry for her." She looked toward the living room where the portrait of Lucy hung above the mantel, thinking how that bright, mischievous face had become so sad. In the silence the children heard the rhythmic creak of the rocking chair.

"Is that you, child?" Auntie's voice crackled out to them. "Come here, child. What have you found?"

"Are you going to tell her?" Betsy jumped up from the step.

"Of course," Amy said, moving toward the living room. "But I have a feeling she already knows."

Grandma had lighted a fire on the huge hearth and Auntie sat before it in the rocker. The flames gave a warm glow to the dim room, their light flickering over the old woman's bony, pale face as she leaned forward to see the children. Betsy stopped in front of the rocker. Amy knelt beside the chair. Only Ben stayed back, drawing close to the far side of the mantel.

"Well, child?"

"Auntie," Amy said, kneeling beside the chair and clasping the gnarled hand between her own warm palms, her voice tight with excitement. "Auntie, Lucy Griffin is here, here in this house still. That's what you meant, isn't it, about old friends. You've met her, too."

"Met her?" Auntie's glance swung up to the mantel, to the pale blur of white that was Lucy Griffin's face. "I know her well. I sit here with her every day, waiting as my father and grandfather did before me."

"No, you don't understand. We've seen her, really, Ben and I. She was there in the attic. I dreamed about her before, but this was different. Please, tell us. It's true that you've seen her, too."

"You've seen her?" Auntie's eyes, hooded in the deeply shadowed sockets of her skull, flashed open, suddenly blue and glinting. She looked at each of the children in turn, then sat forward in the rocker. The sharp points of her fingers dug into Amy's wrist as the old woman pushed slowly up out of the chair and stood in front of the mantel, looking at the portrait.

"What you saw is the gift of the past to the young, from those whose future is unresolved. I had it once, I saw that echo of the past and failed it." There was no anger in her voice, only the ring of sorrow, of abiding loss. She turned to look again at Amy. "You don't understand—I shouldn't have expected that you would. You, child, are the last of her line, the last child of this family until you have children of your own. Her history is your own, and only you can help her."

"I will. I want to. But how?" Amy clutched at the arm of the rocker as though she could wring from it the answers to her family's riddles.

"Her reaching out to us is weakened with each generation. To my knowledge, your grandmother never met her. As a child Louise had no patience with her past. Your father, if he saw, did not accept. But you are like Lucy herself," Auntie said, turning back to the painting. "I knew she would come to you."

"But what does she want? I don't know what to do."

Auntie's gaze slipped back to Amy, then to Ben and to Betsy. For a moment she hesitated, intent on the faces turned toward her. The dim, rainy light sponged her face of its marks of age, and her eyes shone out into the room. She seemed to have shrugged off the frailties of time and stood straight and firm.

"She has very little strength now. She can appear only to those still open to mysteries, to the unknown. But there is not much time."

"You mean she'll go away?" Amy burst out. "Why isn't there time?"

Again the old woman paused, her head tilted to one side as though she listened to a silent voice from the portrait behind her. Then, decided, she held out her hand to Amy.

"Help me to my chair, child." She stepped lightly away from the mantel, moving no longer like a crippled, blind invalid, but with the grace of the young woman she once was. Something had come alive in her, lifting a weight from the frail, aging frame. Settled once more in the rocker, she looked over at Ben.

"Come here, lad, and sit where I can see you. These eyes of mine are fickle in the functioning; not even your discoveries today can restore what time has taken. Sit."

But Ben held back, as though he could not quite believe the transformation of the strange old harridan who had chased him and his sister from the premises several weeks before, into the soft-spoken, glowing person who beckoned to the footstool at her feet.

"Come," she said again.

Reluctantly Ben came over and sat.

"I would not have trusted you," she said to him. "I thought your presence here would bar Lucy's return. But if she sees fit to share her secrets with you, I must not doubt her judgment. Now, in this present, you three share time with her, which I can no longer do. She was like you once, as she is in the portrait, young as I once was. And life changed her as it has changed me, and as it will alter each of you. Some few moments remain to you of childhood, the sweetest and yet the most painful, because you are so near to leaving it. What you will be is complete within you, ready for the use you make of it. And all the doors of decisions not yet made are open to you. Lucy can reach you now; once you step into yourselves completely, there will be no room for her."

Amy opened her mouth to question, but Auntie raised a hand, silencing her.

"That dress you're wearing, Betsy Winters, was my wedding gown. I stitched each seam myself by hand, as I stitched my linens. They were a hateful job to me, the sitting still when spring was blooming, or when the heat of summer called me to the brook. Lucy was my company then. I knew her. Only when I fell to dreaming over where that dress would take me, when each stitch defined the boundaries of my future, only then did I lose her. There is so little time."

"But Auntie," Amy could not help interrupting. "We aren't getting married."

"No. But you are growing up." The old woman smiled and reached out to rub the soft satin of the gown between her thumb and forefinger. "You have other choices open to you; still, they will change you as surely as this wedding gown changed me. If you are to help Lucy Griffin, you must do it soon."

"Then tell us about her."

"Impatience, child, is as common to youth as it is foreign to old age. Let me tell it in my own time, in my own way." Her blue eyes nodded at Amy, but seemed to look backward into a silent, wavering past. Like a clear pool, the room held Auntie's memories swaying in currents around them all.

"I first saw her here in this room. She was smiling, dressed as she is in the portrait. Indeed, for a moment I thought she had stepped down from it, holding her prayer book, but hardly in a mood for catechism. I don't recall that she spoke, yet I knew she was setting off for church to read her lessons with the rector. I wondered at her gaiety; what child has ever willingly passed the first warm days of spring among the musty trappings of faith? But she twirled around in a dance I might have joined, with her muslin skirt spinning around her ankles, then stopped abruptly in answer to some voice I could not hear, and turned toward the hallway. She looked back at me— I could have sworn she winked—before arranging her face in a demure attitude, and vanished.

"I was a child myself, and having wished often for such a playmate, assumed that I had but imagined her. I knew, of course, the stories of Lucy Griffin, knew that she had lived in my room and raised her child on this farm. I had never thought of her as young, though she was not much more than a girl when she married old Charles Griffin and bore his child. It was that hard life my parents cited to me, of the Widow Griffin plowing the fields and chopping ice from the brook in winter for want of a man to help her. But this portrait Lucy, swinging her bonnet, was more real than any of their tales of hardship. Like you, I wanted to know more about her. After that I looked for her. In the late afternoon or early mornings, when the light shifts and glazes our realities with shadow, I sought out quiet places where she might come."

"And did she, Auntie? Did you see her again?" Amy held her breath, waiting for the answer.

"Many times, child. Out among the birches, playing by the brook, I would come upon her. Sometimes she was stand-

ing in the woods, looking up at the treetops. But more often I
would see her on the flat rock in the center of the stream, as
though she were waiting for someone. We didn't speak then,
but she was company for me. I'd offer her tea from acorn cups,
and raspberries served on maple leaf plates. But it was not
always like that."

The children sat, hushed, waiting for Auntie to continue.
She leaned back in the rocker and closed her eyes. After a long
pause, so long that Amy thought she had drifted into sleep,
she sighed and looked up at the portrait.

"One night I awoke abruptly. The moon was full, lighting
the room with a pale, colorless glow. Lucy Griffin stood at the
closed door, her back to me, tugging at the doorknob. As I
watched, she began to pound on the door, calling for her father.
'Let me go,' she cried. 'The war is over. You cannot make me
prisoner to your views for life. Let me go.'

"Suddenly she stepped back and the door opened, but I
could not see into the shadows of the hall. 'He is not a thief,'
she said to her visitor. 'Nor a traitor. It is his right. I shall never
tell you. It is his right, his duty to protect it, as it is my
right to choose to help him.'

"There was a pause, then the door closed again, and Lucy
leaned against it, weeping.

"I lit my lamp, wondering. Had I dreamed it all, dreamed
I was awake? The room was empty, but the memory of Lucy's
sobs stayed with me and saddened me. I got up and stood at
the end of the bed. And she appeared. Her face looked older
to me, not as I imagined she was when she died, but older
than the portrait's Lucy."

"That's how she looked to me," Ben whispered, almost to
himself. "Not really an old woman, but worn-out and
unhappy."

Auntie reached one hand out to him, and Ben took it, holding her fingers lightly on his palm as though he were about to lead her onto the floor to dance.

"Yes, lad, she was unhappy. I would have comforted her, but she raised a hand as though to ward me off. 'Help me,' she said. 'I cannot rest until the legacy is safe.' Now, I had heard of a family legacy from my grandfather, Lucy Griffin's son. He died at ninety when I was twelve, the youngest daughter of his youngest son. He used to tell me tales of riches hidden in the house, silver stolen from the British. My father passed it off as senile prattle, but many's the day I've searched this house in hope of finding treasure. I begged Lucy to tell me where it was. She only shook her head. 'You've seen us by the brook and in among the birches. Where he lies you will find the truth.'

"I didn't understand. 'How can there be truth in lies?' I asked. 'And I've seen only you in the grove by the brook.' Her image wavered then, as though I'd startled her. But she remained and after a moment spoke again. 'History robbed us, let it not blind you. The family tree is how, so seek him out.' I started to question her, but she turned away. 'The family,' she said. 'Acknowledge the family.' And she disappeared."

"That's all?" Amy was disappointed. "That's all she said? And she never came back?"

"I searched the family Bible for some clue as to what she meant."

"And you left it out for me to find, didn't you, Auntie. Was there anything? Did I miss something?"

"No, child, or we both missed something. I memorized the births and deaths and marriages, but it didn't help. I questioned my father, I searched Lucy's room. I even tried to question her further, but it was as though there were a wall between us. Her presence became less and less distinct, her words disconnected. She expected something of me, that I know. But I failed her." The old woman leaned forward and touched the lace at the neckline of the yellowed wedding dress. "And then it was too late. She didn't come back."

Amy sighed. She'd been so sure that Auntie knew a part of the riddle, that together they could solve Lucy Griffin's mystery. "She never mentioned Seth Howes to you?"

"Never! And why should she?" Auntie's face tightened again into the lines of pain and age, and she huddled back in the rocker. "Her father broke with him as soon as the Tory made his politics known. She was a Yankee, child, a heritage this family's taken pride in. That traitor would have no place in her life."

"But why else would she tell me to restore him to his church?"

"She spoke to you? You didn't tell me she spoke to you. What about Seth Howes?"

"Auntie, I don't know. She promised something, and he thinks she betrayed him. Unless we help her, her promise will never be fulfilled. She's waited all these years. If we fail her, she may wait forever. But it has to do with Seth Howes and the church. I thought you'd know what it meant."

"Seth Howes? It's impossible," Auntie murmured. "They were forbidden."

Amy leaned forward on her knees and took Auntie's thin hands in her own. "What does it matter now? She needs our help. I've seen them together there by the brook, on the flat stone. And I think . . . I know they were in love. You heard her say it. A man has a right to protect what he believes, and Lucy had the right to choose between her father's beliefs and the man she loved."

Behind her Amy heard Ben move, reaching out to put his

hand on the worn arm of the rocker. "They did fight that war so that Americans could make up their own minds about their lives, didn't they?"

"And if you trusted Lucy Griffin's judgment of us," Betsy added, "shouldn't you trust her about Seth Howes?"

It was quiet in the room with only the sounds of wood embers crackling in the fireplace, and the beat of rain and wind on the worn clapboard of the old house. At last Auntie raised her head. Her eyes were a faded blue now and tired, but clear.

"Thank you, children. Perhaps it was in my blindness that I failed her."

XIII

Apple Picking

With only two weeks remaining before Halloween, preparations for the party intensified. Once the rector had announced the time and place from the pulpit on Sunday, Grandma was besieged with offers of help. The parish coffee hours on the Sundays preceding the party were busy with planning, with lists and committees and volunteers. While the adults drew up clues for the treasure hunt, the young people were deciding which of the founding fathers to impersonate. In spite of Betsy's insistence, Ben resolutely refused to be Seth Howes, selecting the stubborn Philo Coburn instead. Amy, of course, was to go as Lucy Griffin, and Betsy as her younger sister, Anne. Although at first the boys were not eager to give up their traditional Halloween garb, their enthusiasm mounted with the donations of antique muskets and squirrel-skin caps to the costume committee. After much consultation and digging in each other's caches of old clothes, everyone had a costume. Hat McFee opened her house and her trunks for all to rummage through for headgear, and Mr. Winters pledged a portion of his pumpkin crop for decorations. Even the choirmaster got involved, arranging music for minuets and the Roger de

Coverley, an English country dance popular during colonial times.

To Amy, the weeks before the party passed in a blur of cleaning and baking. Each afternoon when she arrived home from school, Grandma had something different in the oven, giving Amy a chance to sample a variety of pastries while she sat at the kitchen table doing her homework. Grandma insisted on getting down the crystal punch bowl and cups for cider, and had them set on the linen-covered table in the dining room a week ahead of time. And they cleaned. Amy memorized her Latin conjugations while washing the chandelier; Auntie polished the silver, and Grandma scrubbed everything in sight. The old house smelled of ammonia and lemon oil, but the floors and woodwork gleamed, and the antique wood of the tables and chairs glistened. They aired drapes and washed curtains and vacuumed rugs until Auntie declared there would be no nap at all left on them. As each room was completed, Grandma would stand back with a sigh and say, "Now that's the way it looked when I was a child and we had company."

Not only did the house itself respond to this sprucing up, its windows sparkling out on the meadow below, but so did Auntie and Grandma. The fresh fall air, warm with the Indian summer sun, brought color to their cheeks and blew the ache from Auntie's joints. She spoke no more to Amy about the legacy, nor about Lucy Griffin and Seth Howes, seemingly content to leave their fate in Amy's hands. During mealtimes she joined in the conversation about school and enjoyed the bits of gossip Amy brought home from town. She and Grandma chattered at length about where to put the carved pumpkins for the party and supervised Amy's hanging of the orange and black crepe paper streamers in the living and dining rooms.

"They're like two children," Amy said to Ben and Betsy

as they rode to her house together on the bus the day before the party. "Everything is so different from the first day I came, when it all seemed so gray and dark and sad."

"Maybe that was because you were sad," Ben remarked. "You can't have been overjoyed about coming here."

"I wasn't." Only a month ago, Amy realized, she had been a stranger in the old house, awed by Auntie and shy even of her grandmother's love and kindness. But the involvement in school, the regular attendance at church with Grandma, her growing familiarity with the town itself, had drawn her into the community and made her a part of it. Now the ache of homesickness was gone, gone so completely that she had been unaware of the day she had no longer felt it. Like a purple bruise, sore to the touch at first, her pain had faded, swallowed up in the discovery of Lucy Griffin and eased by her friendship with Ben and Betsy. "In fact, I was scared to death to come here," she said.

"You didn't know your grandmother?" Betsy asked.

"Not really. I hadn't seen her since before the war. And I'd never met Auntie. Mom and Dad thought this would be a good chance for me to get acquainted with my relatives. But wait until you see the house," Amy said, changing the subject. "It isn't just my getting used to life here. Everything is different."

The three of them ran up the hill from the bus, eager to get to the orchard to begin picking apples for the apple-bobbing contest. It was a perfect afternoon, crisp and sunny, but smelling of the coming of winter. Leaving Ben in the kitchen with Grandma's doughnuts and a quart of milk, Betsy and Amy hurried upstairs to change their clothes.

"You know," Betsy said, pulling on a pair of jeans, "you really have changed since you came here."

"I have?" Amy stopped rooting through her drawer for

a clean sweater and looked over at her friend. "In what way?"

Betsy thought for a moment. "You aren't as quiet as I thought you were. Not that you're noisy," she amended. "I just thought you were more serious."

"I am serious about some things."

"That's not what I mean." Betsy frowned, then picked up her sweatshirt and pulled it over her head in a quick, brisk motion. "Maybe it's because Ben's been around all the time and we haven't had a chance to talk alone."

"Ben's being around shouldn't make any difference."

"Maybe it shouldn't, but it does. You like him and he likes you," Betsy said in her matter-of-fact way.

"We're friends." Amy bent over to retie her shoes, trying to hide the rush of color to her cheeks. "The three of us are friends."

"It makes a difference," Betsy repeated rather sourly. "Are you ready?"

"Whenever you are," Amy replied. Together they went downstairs and, after fortifying themselves with doughnuts and milk, they slapped out the back door with Ben and up the drive to where Auntie waited for them, seated in a chair in the sunshine at the edge of the orchard. Ben headed for the nearest tree, swinging up on the gnarled old limbs and disappearing into the fading foliage. Betsy scrambled up the tree next in line while Amy got a bushelbasket for the fruit. Looking around the orchard, she saw that most of the trees were barren, having been uncared for since Uncle Plyn's death. She hesitated, feeling vaguely uneasy about her choice, then followed Ben up the tree that seemed to have more ripened fruit than the others. The three picked in silence for a while, rapidly filling the basket. When they could find no more apples easily within reach, Ben slid down and straddled the limb where Amy had placed the basket, his long legs dangling on either side.

"You're right about the house," he said softly. "It feels different, as though it were alive again."

"It's waiting for something, and so is she." Amy looked over at the shawled figure in the sunlight. "We've got to find the legacy, Ben. It means so much to Auntie."

"And to you."

"To all of us." Now that Ben was no longer making fun of her visions, Amy could talk easily to him. All week on the bus they had discussed what they could do to help Lucy. But each had found weaknesses in the other's ideas. Listening to Auntie that Saturday had changed Ben; like Amy, he was now concerned with more than finding a treasure.

"If the legacy is the silver," he said, "what are we going to do with it?"

"Give it back."

"I suppose we have to. But to whom? It doesn't belong to your family, and we can't send it back to England. Who does it belong to?"

"The church, I guess. But there's no sense in worrying about that until we find it."

Ben spotted a gleam of red on the branch above him, pulled down the apple, and rubbed it on his dungarees. "I've been thinking about what your aunt told us the other day, about what Lucy Griffin said to you. It's like one of those puzzles where you have to find the hidden pictures. Maybe we really do have everything in front of us, but we just can't see it."

Amy settled into the wide crotch at the base of the limb on which they sat. "It does seem odd, doesn't it, that Lucy would tell us things we can't understand. You'd think she'd try to make things clearer."

"That's it exactly. I think she has told us everything, maybe so clearly that we don't get it. How well do you remember what she said?"

"Pretty well, I guess."

"Word for word?"

Amy shrugged. "I don't know. They aren't conversations I'd be likely to forget. If Auntie can remember back to what was said seventy years ago, I guess I can remember two or three weeks ago."

"That's what I thought." Ben pulled a piece of notebook paper out of his pocket. It was dirty at the edges and already worn with folding and unfolding. He handed it to Amy. "All week I've been writing down whatever I remember of what you told me, and of what your aunt said on Saturday. Why don't you do the same thing and get her to help you. Then we can compare notes. There must be something we've missed."

"Don't you two do anything but talk?" Betsy peered out from among the branches of the neighboring tree. "If you can't find any apples over there, you can come and help me. And bring the basket. This bag's full."

"Then fill another one," Ben called, tossing his half-eaten apple at her. "This is business."

The apple shot through the branches, just missing Betsy's head. She ducked; the branches shook as she lost her balance and grasped among them to regain it. There was a small cracking sound of twigs breaking behind the veil of leaves, the tree trembled violently, and Betsy came down with a solid thump in the soft, thick grass beneath the tree. Apples from the bag above her head tumbled down, raining around her. She looked so surprised at finding herself on the ground, her hands thrust over her head to ward off the apples, that Ben and Amy burst out laughing.

"It isn't funny." When it was safe to look up, Betsy snatched a rotting windfall from the ground beside her and threw it at them. The apple squashed on the trunk of the tree, its soft pulp splattering and running down the bark. "If it's business, I should be included."

"You're the silent partner." Ben swung down from the tree, scooped up more apples, and began pitching them at his sister. They were soft, partially rotted from lying in the damp, long grass, and they fell around Betsy with soft plops. Ducking them, pitching wildly back at him, she was an easy target.

"Cut it out, you two!" Amy swung down from the tree to stop them, only to be caught in the cross fire. One of Betsy's wild shots hit her in the back as she stepped between them and skidded to her knees on the slippery apple skins. "Come on. That's enough. We'll have to gather them all up again."

Still laughing, Ben stamped through the squashed apples and began helping Amy collect those that had fallen from Betsy's bag. "Get to work, squirt," he said, nudging his sister with his foot. "We were supposed to pick apples, not throw them on the ground."

"You're the one who did the throwing." Betsy stood up and brushed off the seat of her pants. "I'll bet I picked more than the two of you combined. All you've done is talk, talk, talk."

"Ben was just telling me about this idea he had." Rolling an armful of apples into the bushelbasket, Amy began to explain.

"He could have told me, too," Betsy cut in.

"I'm telling you now," Amy said. "It's no big secret. He thought I might remember something important Lucy Griffin had said."

"And I couldn't?"

"Betsy, you weren't even there."

"And neither were you, Ben Winters." Betsy whirled on her brother, her small face tight with hurt and anger.

"But I saw her."

"As if that should make a difference. You two think you're so great just because you saw her and I didn't. You whisper on the bus, and now you're passing notes back and forth and laughing at me." She snapped around to face Amy. "I thought you were my friend. But if this is the way you treat your friends, you can keep your friendship to yourself. And you can solve your old mystery without me!"

She spun on her heel and stalked off, out of the orchard and down the hill toward the meadow and the path toward home.

"Betsy, wait." Amy started after her, stumbling on the fallen apples. Betsy's pace never slowed, nor did she look back. In a moment she was out of sight in the birch grove. Ben caught Amy's arm.

"Let her go. She'll cool off. She never could take a little teasing."

"Shouldn't you go after her and tell her we're sorry?"

"For what? I'm the one who threw the apples. You didn't do anything."

"Yes, I did," Amy said. "I didn't listen. She was trying to tell me today how she felt, and I didn't even hear her." Amy turned away from Ben and looked down the hill. It isn't the apples Betsy's angry about, she thought. It was bad enough for her to be the only one of the partnership, which now included Auntie, who had not experienced the presence of either Lucy Griffin or Seth Howes. The real insult was to be excluded, not from the past, but from the present, as though Ben's growing friendship with Amy had replaced her own. Amy knew that hurt, the sense of being abandoned by someone you thought cared about you. She cringed inside, recalling how she had ignored Betsy during the past week.

"Forget it, Amy. She won't stay mad, honest."

"But I don't blame her for being angry."

"If it will make you feel any better, I'll apologize," Ben said, still holding her arm and looking closely at her.

"It isn't your fault." Amy shivered. Already the mists were rising in the valley, and the warm afternoon had dropped suddenly into evening. The shadows deepened through the orchard, casting long clumps of darkness down into the meadow. All the excitement, all the fun, had gone out of the party preparations with Betsy's departure, and Amy felt both dejected and responsible.

"We'd better go," she said. "Auntie will be chilled through."

"Whatever you say. I'll put the apples on the porch and get our things." Ben picked up the bushelbasket. "And if you need any more help, call me. See you tomorrow."

Amy watched him leave, then walked slowly over to the edge of the orchard. Auntie looked up at the sound of her footsteps. "What's the matter? Finished already?"

"I'm afraid so." Amy sat on the wide arm of the lawn chair and looked down the long stretch of meadow to the valley. After a few moments Auntie pulled the shawl closer around her shoulders and cleared her throat.

"It's comforting, isn't it," she said, "to see the lights blink on as the valley darkens."

"You can see that?"

"No, but I know it's there. I can't see your face either, but I know you're unhappy."

"Betsy's mad at me, at me and Ben. She probably won't even speak to me tomorrow."

"So, the changes begin already."

"Changes?"

"Awareness is a better word. Being aware of complexities, making choices, are part of the process of becoming an adult."

"I didn't choose to hurt Betsy's feelings. I told Ben to tell her I was sorry."

"You did make a choice, intentionally or not. And being sorry isn't enough."

"What can I do? I can't take back the way we acted."

"No, child, you can't change what has happened, only what will happen. And that will depend on both you and Betsy. Though our futures spring from the past, blessedly they aren't shackled to it."

"But suppose she stays mad, Auntie? I've lost a friend."

"Good friends are not so easily dismissed." Auntie stood up and slid her hand into the crook of Amy's arm, squeezing gently. "Betsy is hurt now. Showing her you're sorry will mean more than a thousand apologies, and your friendship will be the stronger for it. Do you know your Scriptures, child?"

"Not very well."

" 'Be ye angry and sin not; let not the sun go down upon your wrath,' " Auntie quoted.

"It's too late for that." Amy looked over her shoulder at the crest of mountains where the sun had disappeared.

"Too late for Lucy Griffin, with all her suns set," the old woman said softly, returning again to the theme of all her conversations with Amy. "She waited too long to forgive her family, this town, for the grudge she harbored. Generations of wrath have kept her from her rest. It blinded me, and I could not help her. But not too late for you, nor for me either, old as I am. Learn from the past, child, learn from it."

Abruptly she squared her shoulders and tugged sharply at Amy's arm. "Come along now, it's getting late. Your grandmother will be looking for us."

Later Amy sat at the small table in her room listening to the night sounds of the house. There was a heaviness in the air, and she was restless, still worrying about Betsy. The rupture in their friendship was unsettling, as everything in her life seemed to be lately. She slouched down in the chair, jamming her hands in her pockets, and felt the paper Ben had given her. Opening it, she saw that there were only five or six sentences written down, mostly attributed to Auntie's memory.

"Help me," read the first. "I cannot rest until the legacy is safe." Then, "You've seen us by the brook. His lies are truth." Amy penciled an X beside that one to check with Auntie. It did not seem to be exactly as Auntie had reported it, though Ben had put it in quotes. Lower down on the page he had written, "Blinded by history. Acknowledge the family, the family tree."

Under her own name, Amy saw that Ben had recorded Lucy's request that Seth Howes be returned to his church. She read and reread the sentences, then took out her own piece of notebook paper and began to write, trying to remember exactly what Seth had said to her in the church, as well as what Lucy had said. When she was satisfied that it was as close to accurate as she could make it, she folded the two pieces of paper together and tucked them into the cover of the family Bible. Tomorrow, she thought as she crawled under the heavy patchwork quilt, tomorrow was soon enough to check the wording, and then to ask Betsy her advice. She closed her eyes and was asleep.

XIV

Halloween Party

By evening the preparations for the party were complete, even to Grandma's nervous, all-noting eye. The dining room table was set with trays of cookies, tarts, and small cakes decorated with orange and black frosting. An arrangement of colored leaves, gourds, Indian corn, and small pumpkins formed the centerpiece on the creamy, white linen cloth, and tall brass candlesticks gleamed at each end of the table in the flickering light of their tapers. Strips of orange and black crepe paper were strung across the ceiling, and cornstalks and pumpkins were arranged in the corners of the room. In the living room the furniture had been pushed up against the walls or removed altogether, the rugs were rolled, and the choirmaster had set up his harpsichord to provide music for dancing. Candles and kerosene lamps, carefully set at a distance from the flammable decorations, illuminated the two main rooms of the house with a pale, golden glow that set off the burnished woodwork and floors. Amy could hardly wait for the evening to begin and stood impatiently while Grandma finished plaiting her hair into the style of Lucy Griffin's. Finally she stepped back.

"There!" Grandma crossed her arms over the flaming red

gypsy blouse that was part of her fortuneteller's costume and nodded. "You're the picture of a picture, and that's for sure. It's uncanny how you resemble that portrait, Amy, and after all these generations of Griffins and non-Griffins between you and Lucy."

"Blood will tell." Auntie tapped into the room, leaning on her cane. "Stand in the light, child, and let me get a look at you. Indeed," she said, peering closely at Amy through the thick glasses, "to these blurring eyes, you could be Lucy Griffin herself."

"A shawl," Grandma said, tapping her forefinger on her lips. "She needs a shawl. You wait here and listen for the Winterses' car, and I'll see what I have in the cedar chest."

"The Winterses? You called them?"

"You don't think I'd let you walk alone to the church at night? They should be along any minute. I'll be right back."

"Auntie, what will I do? Suppose Betsy won't talk to me?"

"You'll talk to her. That's all you can do." Auntie's fingers traced the smooth weave of Amy's braids. "No sense in worrying about it now. It will work out, or it won't."

"I suppose so." Amy considered for a minute, then took from the pocket of her apron the page of notes and additions she had made to Ben's list. "But whatever happens I'm going to give her this. It's about Lucy Griffin. Ben had this idea. I meant to ask you about it last night. At first I wasn't sure, but now I think he's right. Please read it. Maybe you'll see it, too."

She unfolded the paper and started to hand it to Auntie, but the old woman motioned it away. "I'm long past seeing words on a page, child, unless I already know what they are."

"But you do know. We've written down everything Lucy Griffin has told us. It's the way we think about what she's said that changes everything."

Quietly Amy began reading the quotations, ending with the chant she had heard in her room. "The key . . . L . . . M . . . how's her name."

" 'How's her name,' " Auntie repeated, then looked sharply at Amy. "And what's this about a key? You never mentioned a key before."

"I thought you knew and were just waiting for me to find it. Until last night, when I started writing everything down, I didn't think about telling you. So much else was happening. It's here." Quickly Amy removed the acorn top of the bedpost and laid the tiny key in Auntie's palm. "Do you know what lock it fits?"

Auntie sat down heavily at the desk, her gnarled fingers curling tightly over the key. For a moment she was perfectly still, her eyes closed. Then she turned back to Amy.

"I can't remember," she said, shaking her head. "It was so long ago. Maybe there was something, but it's too late, child. I'm too old to help you."

"You're not, Auntie. Please don't say that." Amy knelt by the old woman, touched by the paper-thin despair in her voice. "Without you there would have been nothing. I'd have thought it was all a dream."

"An old woman's dream. Because I was wrong about so many things. But you'll find the answers, child, I know you will." She reached out and brushed Amy's cheek in a feathery caress. "The car is here. Go on now, and enjoy your evening."

Impulsively Amy leaned forward and hugged the old woman, planting a quick kiss on her wrinkled cheek. "I'll try, Auntie. And you enjoy it, too. I'll see you later."

Amy was halfway down the stairs when she saw Ben in the hallway. He was wrapped in the black wool cloak from the attic, his hair was streaked with gray, and he'd drawn in a mustache and sideburns on his face with burnt cork. He glanced up, startled, as Amy appeared out of the shadowy stairwell.

"Return Seth Howes to his church," Amy crooned, mimicking Lucy, "else I cannot rest."

Ben's eyes widened, and he seemed about to bolt from the room. Instead, he squared his shoulders, took a deep breath, and whispered, "We can't help you unless we understand."

Amy took a step closer. "Ben, it's me, Amy. Don't you recognize me? Do I look that much like Lucy Griffin?"

"In the dark you do." Ben gave a little shiver and looked from Amy to the dimly lit portrait in the living room. "You sure gave me a start. You might have let me know right off that it was you."

"I thought you'd realize." Amy ran down the last couple of steps. "Is Betsy still mad at me?"

"You'll have to ask her yourself. She isn't talking much to me. Come on. She and Dad are waiting for us in the car."

Amy kissed her grandmother good-by and, wrapped in the white crocheted shawl, followed Ben out to the driveway. Betsy was sitting in the front seat next to her father.

"Hello, Mr. Winters," Amy said as she climbed into the back seat with Ben. "Hi, Betsy."

"Hi." Betsy continued looking straight ahead. Mr. Winters put the car in gear and swung out of the driveway and down Bridge Street. The trees along the side of the road, their limbs nearly bare of leaves now, stretched up in unmoving silhouettes against the night sky. Clouds scudded swiftly across the face of the full moon, blotching its light, giving Amy the impression that the moon itself was racing toward the far horizon while the earth reeled in the opposite direction. It was a dizzying sensation, as though the physical rules of the universe had suddenly reversed themselves.

"It's a good night for ghosts and goblins," Mr. Winters

said, breaking the silence. "Warm for the end of October. It's the kind of weather that brews storms behind these mountains. That's something for you to see, Amy, when the clouds break over this valley. I wouldn't be surprised to see some rain before this night's out."

"If that last rain was any sample, I hope it waits until the treasure hunt is over. We'd really get soaked."

"And flooded out as well. That brook above the church has been known to wash out the main road." He pulled into the church parking lot. "Here you are. Call me when you're ready to come home, kids, and behave yourselves."

Betsy hopped out quickly and walked ahead of Ben and Amy toward the church steps. The headlights of the car swung past the children, lighting their faces for an instant, then leaving them in the glow of the fleeting moonlight. Betsy's face was set in a determined frown.

"Wait," Amy said as they reached the door of the church. "Betsy, I'm sorry about yesterday. I didn't mean to ignore what you were saying or to shut you out of everything. We need your help. Please read this." She fumbled in her apron pocket for the envelope.

Betsy hesitated, then took the note. "You don't have to make a special effort on my account."

"I think I do," Amy replied. "I want us to be friends, so it's important for you to know I'm sorry. But that's between you and me. This is about Lucy Griffin."

"There's something new?"

"Not really. I think I just noticed something that's been there all along. Read the note and we can talk later." Amy pulled open the door and went into the church.

Although the altar was bare and unlit, the interior of the church glowed with lights along the aisles of the nave. The stained-glass windows seemed to absorb the light in their rich colors, reducing it and altering its quality so that it reflected, pearllike, in the painted pews and walls. Seen from the inside, with the night black behind them, the windows seemed denser, thicker, and flatter. Their deeper hues transformed the ordinary, daylight appearance of the church, tinging it with an aura of mystery that matched the mood of the night. The building's shadowed reaches were remote and hushed, yet the air was charged with the excitement of the young people who were already gathered for the treasure hunt. Dressed as their own ancestors, people long departed from this earth, they wriggled and whispered in the pews, their voices bristling in anticipation of the evening's activities. Heads turned as Ben, Betsy, and Amy entered and were waved toward seats beside their friends. Sweeping his cape back over one shoulder, Ben gallantly escorted the girls down the aisle, grinning in response to the muffled snickers and comments of his friends. At Philo Coburn's pew he stopped, opened the gate, and bowed Betsy and Amy to their seats. He hesitated a moment, drawn by the signals of his regular gang, then saluted them with a wide sweep of his hat and slipped into the pew next to Betsy. For the next few minutes, as others continued to arrive, they greeted one another and commented on the variety of costumes. There were colonists of all rank, from white-wigged aristocrats to straw-hatted farmers, and even one Salem witch complete with blacked-out teeth. At last the rector arrived, and they all settled down to listen to the directions for the treasure hunt.

"The first order of business is to divide you up into teams," the rector said, taking out a folded paper from his pocket. "I'll give each group this first clue and send you off in intervals of five minutes. Whichever group arrives at the Griffin place in the shortest time, wins. And anyone who hasn't found the last clue within an hour of starting had better give up and go on to the farm or you'll miss the cider and doughnuts! Remember, we're celebrating the anniversary of the founding of this parish. Those of you who know your history should have no problem following the clues. Just be sure you replace each one for the next group." He handed the note to the boy sitting nearest him. "Here you go, Bill. Good luck, now."

Awaiting their turn, Betsy opened Amy's note. Amy tried not to watch her face as she read, concentrating instead on the stained-glass windows and the bronze plaques that were set on the church walls in honor of loyal parishioners. From the corner of her eye she saw Betsy push her glasses up on her nose and hold the paper out so Ben could read over her shoulder. Her eyebrows wrinkled together as she read it a second time.

"Howes?" she murmured, looking up at Amy. "Howes is her name?"

"It's logical, isn't it?"

Ben nodded. "But that doesn't tell us where the silver is, or what it has to do with the legacy."

"But it does. Remember that she told Auntie to acknowledge the family? And here, Ben, where you wrote that Seth lied, Lucy told Auntie she'd find the truth 'where Seth lies.' Don't you see?"

"You mean she buried the legacy with him?"

"If she did," Betsy said, "we'll never get it."

"If she had, the whole town would have known about it," Amy said. "The answer has to be in the family history. She talked about a family tree. Maybe that's the right track."

Just then a shadow fell over the paper. The rector leaned over and handed Ben the first clue to the treasure hunt.

"Your turn now. Read it carefully."

Amy stuffed her envelope back into her apron pocket and listened as Ben read the clue aloud.

"'Thomas Brown first struck it.
  To him it paid full toll.

Who seeks on high will find it,
And bring home first the goal.' "

"Thomas Brown? Who's he?" Ben looked blankly at the girls. "And what or who do you suppose he struck?"

" 'On high,' " Betsy mused. "That could be the organ, or . . . of course, the belfry! Thomas Brown was the man who cast the bell. Come on."

They tumbled out of the pew, ran to the back of the church and up the stairs to the choir loft. Hiking up her skirts, Betsy began to climb the roughly hewn ladder that led to the tower of the church. The beams of the old building were dark with age, rubbed smooth where generation after generation had used them as handholds. Betsy stepped onto the platform and looked up at the huge bell.

"Now all we have to do is find the clue," Ben said, clambering up onto the platform beside her while Amy scrambled up the ladder behind him. "You're sure about Thomas Brown?"

"There's his name, right there," Betsy said, pointing to the rim of the bell. "And the date, I think, though it's pretty hard to see up here."

Floodlights on the lawn lit the church steeple so that people passing on the main road could see the time on the old clock face. Melding with the moonlight, the beam shone through the louvers of the belfry, casting a lattice pattern on the bell and its frame. A thick coil of rope ran from the top of the bell down one side of the tower to the main floor of the church.

"When Thomas Brown died," Betsy continued, "they rang the bell once for each year of his life, so it paid him full toll. This must be right, but I don't see any clue."

"Is that it?" Amy pointed to a glimmer of white stuck to the beam above Ben's head. As Ben reached for it, Amy stepped back against the wall to give him room. Through the louvers she could see the town and the eastern side of the valley. Directly below them was the churchyard. Amy gazed down, watching the movement of moonlight and shadow across the old stone markers.

" 'From heights to depths,' " she heard Ben read, and she turned from the view to listen to him.

" 'From heights to depths the soul must go.' "

The griffin in its flight also.

Seek out where the griffin lies.

This step will lead you to the prize.' "

"I give up. What's a griffin?" Ben asked, looking up from the paper. "These are tough clues."

"It's one of those half and half creatures," Betsy said. "You know, half bird, half horse, something like that."

"It would help if we knew exactly."

"I think it's a lion and an eagle," Amy said. "I know it has wings. But the clue must mean the Griffin plot. There aren't any gargoyles on this church, are there, Betsy? Sometimes griffins are carved as decorations on buildings."

"None that I know of. That must be right. Come on. Let's go."

As Ben started down the ladder, Amy glanced again through the louvers. She expected to see figures there, of the groups that had gone before them, but at first there was nothing except the flickering shadows of the moonlight. Not until Betsy's head was disappearing down the ladder after Ben did Amy see anyone.

"Wait!" she cried. "Look!"

In an instant Betsy was beside her at the louver.

"Look, down there by the fence. It's Seth Howes."

Betsy peered out, squinting down at the churchyard. "Are you sure? I don't see anyone. Where is he, Amy?"

"Right there, in the shadow of the elm. There, by the fence."

"Maybe it's just the shadow of the elm."

Amy nudged her aside and looked again. For a moment she thought he was gone. Then, at a break in the clouds, the full light of the moon fell over the churchyard and she saw the tall, spare figure moving slowly among the markers.

"He's there. Quickly. We've got to talk to him."

She swung around to the ladder and started down, her skirts tangling around her legs. Ben was waiting at the head of the stairs.

"What took you so long?"

"It's Seth Howes. He's here, in the churchyard." She rushed past Ben, down the stairs and out the front door of the church. Cold air struck her face, and the smell of rain. Mr. Winters was right, she thought as she ran across the lawn toward the churchyard. The wind was blowing now, massing clumps of heavy cumulus clouds that blotted out the stars. Behind her she heard Ben's and Betsy's footsteps on the gravel. She rounded the corner of the church and, dodging among the markers, headed toward the Griffin plot. She saw no one, heard no one, and briefly wondered where the other treasure hunters were. At the foot of Lucy Griffin's grave she paused.

"Seth? Seth Howes, where are you?"

There was no answer, only the sound of the rising wind. Heavy clouds roiled over half the sky, deepening the shadows.

"Where is he?" Ben panted. "Did you catch up with him?"

"He's gone, Ben, if he was ever really there. I can't even be sure of that now. It's so dark."

Betsy came up beside them, turning to look back over her shoulder. "I don't like this. Where are the others? They should be around here somewhere."

The wind caught her voice, snatching away pieces of words.

Suddenly she grabbed Amy's arm and pointed off to the left toward the elm tree in the field. A man stood there, his black coat torn back by the wind, the ends of the wide tie at his throat whipped back over his shoulders. He was looking up the hill to the old farmhouse where glimmers of yellow light showed at the windows.

"Seth," Amy called again, funneling her hands around her mouth against the wind. "Seth Howes."

If he heard, Seth gave no sign. He remained standing by the tree, distinguishable under the now black sky only by the white, streaming tie. Amy started to run forward, but Ben held her back.

"Where are you going?" he shouted at her above the rush of wind through branches. Far off on the horizon there was a flash of lightning, followed by a low rumble of thunder.

"We've got to talk to him, Ben. Come on."

"He can't even hear us. It'll be pouring in a few minutes. We'd better go up to the house."

"The others must have gone on already." Betsy glanced around the deserted churchyard. "Please, Amy, let's go. I don't like this. There's nobody left around, and even the clue is gone. Maybe they called everything off. We couldn't have heard them from up in the belfry."

"The clue probably blew away." Amy pulled her shawl closer around her. The storm clouds were heavier now, their billowing contours revealed by the more frequent slashes of lightning. The entire sky seemed to have lowered over the valley, pressing down on the tops of the trees. The figure of Seth Howes remained beside the elm, but he was leaning forward into the wind. Large drops of rain began to bounce off the stone grave markers, and Amy felt them splat against her cheek. She looked at Ben and Betsy, their pale, worried faces gleaming with moisture.

"Don't you see?" she cried. "If we don't solve this thing now, they may have to wait another whole generation. And then it may be too late. It will certainly be too late for Auntie." She hesitated, then stepped away from them. "You go on to the house. I'll talk to him alone. I'm not afraid."

"What will you say?"

"I don't know, Ben, but I've got to see him once more. I know he'll talk to me."

"You aren't going alone," Betsy said firmly. "Either we all go, or we all stay."

"Then let's go," Ben said. "But stay together."

They started across the churchyard, stumbling in the rain-swept darkness. At the fence Amy stopped. Seth was gone from the tree, walking with long strides up the hill toward the farm and the grove of birches. She swung over the fence, shouting after him. "Seth, Seth Howes, wait!"

Once in the meadow, Ben took the lead, angling up the hill. The rough grass caught on the girls' long skirts, and the wind twisted the material around their legs. The top branches of the old elm were bent sharply by the storm, and small branches broke and fell, cracking underfoot.

"He's too fast for us," Ben said, slowing to let Amy and Betsy catch up. "I can't tell which way he's going."

There was a crack of lightning followed almost immediately by a long crash of thunder. The rain hissed from the clouds, coming in sharp, needle-pointed drops. Ben grabbed Amy's hand and pulled her along behind him on the faint path to the farm. Betsy trailed after them, her skirts hiked up to her knees. At the crest of the hill Ben stopped again.

"He's gone."

"No." Amy pressed the ache in her side and tried to catch her breath. "He saw the lights in the house. He'd go to the rock in the brook. It's just a little farther, through the birches."

Once in the birch grove, they found the going easier. Amy ran ahead toward the brook. Already it sounded fuller, rushing to meet the rain that was pouring into the valley. Amy dodged through the trees, searching among their white trunks for the black-cloaked figure with the flutter of white at his throat. Thunder sounded again as they neared the edge of the brook. Ben and Betsy scrambled up behind her.

"This is no place to be in a thunderstorm," Ben muttered. "He's got more sense than we have. He's gone."

"No, wait. Look there, upstream." Amy pointed to the rock some dozen yards ahead of them, though the rain and darkness made the gesture almost useless. "He's there."

Slipping at the very edge of the water, Amy made her way toward the rock. When she was directly parallel to it she stopped again and called.

"Seth? Seth Howes."

He turned to face her. Beaconed by the recurrent flashes of light, which seemed to catch and reflect from the brook and the birches, his face was clear to her. He stared at Amy, then shook his head.

"Do not deceive me again. Is not her betrayal enough?"

"But she did not betray you. She's trying to help you still."

"She denied her promise and her name."

"No. Howes is her name," Amy shouted over the wind and rain. "On the stone. Howes is her name in the sight of God. She tried to tell us, to tell you."

For a moment the heavy lines of his face lifted, but again he shook his head. "It cannot be. The legacy I left with her, the promise she made, goes unfulfilled."

"The silver? The communion silver?"

"I left it in her trust."

"She wants us to find it for you."

But Seth's eyes were no longer on Amy. He saw Ben and

Betsy at the stream's bank and raised his arm, pointing at them.

"Leave me," he cried, his voice carrying over the violence of the storm. "I will have no more of your treachery. Those who would deny their king would deny also their God. I want no part of your blasphemy."

"Wait, you don't understand." Amy reached out, stepping forward. Her foot slipped into the rising brook, and she nearly fell headlong into the stream, saved only by Ben's grabbing her and pulling her back. The rain was pounding down in sheets now, beating on the rocks, water, and trees. She scrambled back onto the bank and looked up, wiping the rain from her face, but Seth Howes was gone.

"What was that last bit about?" Betsy asked, her hand clenched on Amy's arm. "He doesn't sound too friendly."

"He thought you were colonists, I guess, patriots. He wouldn't say anything about the silver to you, or to me either now."

"He's said all he's going to say tonight. Let's go, Amy. We're drenched. Your grandmother's going to have a fit." Ben took her hand again and, with Betsy leading the way, they started back through the grove toward the house.

A haven of light and warmth on the bleak, rain-swept hillside, the house offered them shelter from the weather and the promise of hot food and drink. Lights from the windows sent yellow rectangles out onto the lawn and driveway, and the clear, trembling notes of the harpsichord pierced the noise of the storm as they approached. Through the living room window, in the light of the huge hearth and the lamps and candles, they could see young people in colonial costume moving through the measured steps of a minuet, smiling and nodding in time to the music. For an instant it seemed to Amy as if Seth Howes's was the true reality, that she and Ben and Betsy had moved back completely into his time. Only the solid thump of their footsteps on the wooden front porch, the sight of the cars in the driveway, the twinkling of lights from houses in the valley, and the continued steady grip of Ben's hand around her own, snapped her world into perspective. Dripping wet, she and Ben and Betsy burst into the vestibule. The bright lights and warm air, the noise of the party, stunned them momentarily. Then the faces of the present came into focus, the concerned and familiar faces of friends and family. The unreal atmosphere of the storm fell away, replaced by the comforting solidity of the house itself, the reassuring bulk of dining room table and sideboard, the physical presence of the guests. The party decorations stood out in stark contrast to the swirling rain and wind beyond the door, and the fragrances of food and hot cider were tantalizingly vivid. Everything was incredibly vivid to Amy, clear and palpable. She noticed minute details, observed items as though she had never looked at them before. She felt the wetness of her shoes, the icy cold of Betsy's fingers on her arm, and watched the slow smearing of Ben's sideburns as the rain dripped out of his hair and down his cheeks. It was all wonderfully tangible and as reassuring as the starchy smell of Grandma's apron as she enveloped Amy in a hug.

"Amy! Amy, where have you been?" Grandma held her close then at arm's length to see that she was not hurt. "When no one remembered seeing you, we were worried sick that you'd been lost in this storm. And look, you're soaking wet, the three of you. Surely you weren't following those silly clues all this time?"

"The last one blew away on us, Mrs. Enfield," Ben said. "And it was rough walking against that wind. I hope you saved us some cider and doughnuts."

"It's hot punch for you, young man. Whatever would your mother think of me, Amy, if she could see you now!" She mopped at Amy's face with a fold of the voluminous gypsy skirt.

"We're just a little wet."

"A little! Then come and get a little dry while I get you something hot to drink to take the chill off." As she spoke, Grandma was gathering up the dripping shawl, Ben's cloak, and Betsy's scarf. "Take those wet shoes off and Amy, you take Betsy upstairs to change. You must have something that will fit her. Thank goodness you weren't hit by lightning."

"Where's Auntie?"

"Telling stories by the fire. You can join her as soon as you change. Go on now." She shooed them off and bustled away to the kitchen, calling out as she passed through the dining room, "It's all right, everyone, they're here. They're safe."

XV

The Storm

"Now that was a party!" Grandma exclaimed to Auntie, Amy, and the Winterses, flopping down on the couch in the living room. The other guests had left, and the litter of the party had been picked up and stashed in big brown grocery bags in the kitchen. Orange napkins and paper coffee cups, paper plates and candy wrappers, and fallen black and orange streamers had been gathered up from the floor and window sills, from the tabletops and mantelpiece. The crystal cups and punch bowl and the cookie platters were on the kitchen counter for washing in the morning. In the corners of the dining room the cornstalks drooped over Mr. Winters's pumpkins, and the candles on each side of the centerpiece on the table were burned to nubs in their shiny brass holders.

Mr. Winters and Ben had unrolled the rugs in the living room and replaced most of the furniture, returning the room to normal. Only the Indian corn on the mantel, the basket of polished apples and the grinning jack-o'-lantern on the hearth, and the heap of hot embers in the fireplace remained to mark the occasion. Tired but happy with the success of the evening, Grandma leaned back and mopped her face with a leftover napkin, smearing the heavy gypsy make-up in dark streaks above her eyebrows, which gave her a quizzical expression. "I haven't had that much fun in years," she said.

"I haven't either, Grandma. Can we do it again next year?"

"I certainly hope so, dear." Grandma smiled, but a catch in her voice reminded Amy that her visit was a temporary one, and that Grandma and Auntie could not plan too far into the future.

"If we are going to do it again," Ben said, "you're going to have to practice apple bobbing. It's against the rules to bite the stem."

"It's probably against the rules to dive into the tub, too," Amy replied, laughing as she recalled Ben's submersion. "It certainly finished off your mustache!"

"Which made him no less attractive a partner in the Virginia reel, I noticed," Grandma said. "What memories that brought back, seeing you young folks dancing."

"It was fun, too," Ben admitted, grinning at Amy. His hair hung in a tangled clump over his forehead, the white tie of his costume swung in a knot around his neck, and his white stockings sagged loosely around his ankles. Though he couldn't be described as handsome, Amy thought, returning his smile, Ben had his own special charm. Dancing with him, spinning arm and arm through the steps of the reel, had been a gay and fitting conclusion to the evening. The music and laughter, the colorful colonial costumes and Halloween decorations, the very crowding of the guests into rooms so long deserted, had given the old homestead new life. For a few hours it had shed its weight of painful memories and shared in the merriment of a new generation, reflecting the pleasures of the past—of Lucy Griffin's youth, and Auntie's and Grandma's—in those of the present. Thinking of those long-ago parties, Amy turned and looked up at the portrait.

"There, see!" Betsy hopped up from her place on the stool

at the foot of Auntie's rocker and held a kerosene lamp up to the painting. "They could be the same person."

"But they are not," Auntie murmured, so softly that only Amy heard. "You are each yourselves, with your own futures."

"Future?" Ben asked. "What about the future? I never did get my fortune told, Mrs. Enfield. How about reading my palm now?"

"Even I could tell your immediate future," Mr. Winters said. "You will take a short trip down a steep hill to a familiar structure where you will be wrapped in soft blankets for an unspecified time. That is, we'll take you home and put you to bed until you wake up."

"It has been a busy evening." Grandma sat up and looked at Auntie, who was rocking slowly in her chair. "Matilda, you must be exhausted. Whatever were you telling those children? They were utterly fascinated. I wouldn't be surprised if they came up to see you every day all winter long!"

"We were talking about the old days. It helps me to remember."

Amy glanced quickly at her, but if Auntie had recalled something about Lucy Griffin or the legacy, it did not show in her face. Mr. Winters stood up.

"I think it's time we got home and let these people go to bed." He paused, listening to the beat of the rain on the windows, the rattle of branches on the porch roof as the wind bent the old elm over the house. "That's a bad storm, Mrs. Enfield," he said to Grandma. "Sure you won't come down with us and spend the night? We've plenty of room."

"This house has weathered many a storm," Auntie said. "We'll be quite safe here."

"And there's always the phone if we need anything," Grandma added. "No need to worry about us."

"Just the same, remember we're there if you need us."

They gathered up their things, including bags of extra doughnuts and cookies that Grandma insisted on sending with them, and said their goodnights.

"I'll call you tomorrow," Betsy whispered to Amy at the door. "Be sure to tell your aunt what happened tonight. Maybe she can fit things together. And Amy," she added, "thanks for including me tonight, for making that special effort. I guess I was a little jealous of you and Ben."

"It was my fault. I'm just awfully glad that we're friends again, all three of us. I'll talk to you tomorrow."

As soon as they were gone, Amy returned to the living room. Grandma had extinguished the lamps, and the flickering light from the jack-o'-lantern and the dying fire gave an eerie tone to the room, emphasized by the regular creak of Auntie's chair. Gusts of wind swirled around the house, causing yellow flames to burst unexpectedly from the blue tendrils of fire that hovered over the red coals. Auntie rocked steadily, seemingly oblivious to Amy, to the room itself, and to the storm that battered the house. So deep was her concentration that Amy hesitated to interrupt her. She stood in the doorway, watching, until Grandma came up behind her and switched on the lights. As the sudden brightness illuminated the room, Auntie stopped rocking and looked up, first at Amy, and then at the portrait over the mantel. All three of them stared at it for a moment, startled by the effect of the sudden bright light. For the first time Amy saw, really saw, the small black book that Lucy held in her hand in the painting. It was a black leather prayer book with a gold cross on the cover, and Lucy's right thumb was pointed directly at the gold clasp that held it closed, a gold clasp with a tiny keyhole at its center.

Before Amy could point it out, before she could say anything at all, Grandma was hustling her off to bed.

"Just blow out the jack-o'-lanterns," she said, "and go

on to bed. We can take care of everything else tomorrow. The witching hour is past for this year, and it's time I got you two settled in for the night. It won't take me long to get to sleep tonight, that's for sure."

In spite of the excitement of the evening, Amy could not remain awake either. She burrowed down beneath the heavy quilts, planning to think about the prayer book and where it might be, and about Seth Howes's latest appearance. She closed her eyes, feeling her breath warm against the sheets she had snuggled up around her nose, and her last thought was of the locked book in Lucy's lap.

Hours later she awoke, as suddenly as she had fallen asleep. The storm still pummeled the valley with rain, and the wind made a deeply pitched, droning sound. But it was not that which had awakened Amy, nor was it the rumbles of thunder and cracks of lightning. She sat up, listening. One of the shutters had come loose and was banging against the house, and branches scraped the roof. Amy got out of bed and looked out the window. Small and medium-sized branches were scattered on the porch roof and on the lawn below, and the big elm seemed permanently twisted by the strong wind. Then Amy heard it again, a faint, distant voice. She turned and ran to the door of her room, pulling it open. The hallway was dark, the closed door of her grandmother's room a more palpable blackness. But Auntie's room was open. Amy listened again, then padded softly downstairs to the living room.

Auntie stood in front of the portrait, leaning on her cane, murmuring something Amy could not make out. Her hair, usually bound up in a bun at the back of her neck, hung down, streaming whitely on the dark shawl she had wrapped around her shoulders.

"Auntie, what is it?" Amy crossed the room and touched her aunt's arm. "Are you all right?"

"The book, child, it is the book we need. My grandfather told us she had hidden the book with the family tree." She turned to Amy, gripping her shoulders with bony strength. "You have the key. You must find the book."

"Of course, Auntie, we will." Gently Amy helped the old woman to sit down in the rocking chair, trying to calm her. Although she spoke in an even voice and had stood firmly, her whole body exuded a frightening tension, an agitation that was near the breaking point. "Please sit down, Auntie. I'll get Grandma. She'll make you a cup of tea."

"I don't want a cup of tea. Listen to me, child. She told us but we didn't understand. It is just as you said. We heard only the words." She leaned toward Amy, speaking rapidly in her whispery voice so that Amy barely heard her over the crashing of wind and rain outside. "Lucy herself told me, and you. The family tree is not what's written in the Bible. And your 'L . . . M' is not a person."

A gust of wind banged against the house, rattling the windows and sending a shower of branches and shingles down from the roof. Both Amy and Auntie looked up. For an instant there was silence, as though the storm had paused to gather up its strength. Then a blinding bolt of light filled the room, making it shadowless, washing out all color with its brilliance. At the same time a deafening crash split the air with a force that made the house shudder, then rolled away into a steady roar of thunder.

"The tree!" Auntie sprang up from the rocker, pushing Amy aside. Her cane swung forward, pointing toward the window, then fell to the floor. Auntie stepped back, reaching for Amy. She tried to speak, but no sound came. Horrified,

Amy saw her crumple forward as though the support of bone and muscle had suddenly failed her, leaving only the clothes she wore to define her being. Amy reached out in time to catch the frail weight as Auntie fell to the floor.

"Auntie," she cried. "Auntie!"

The old woman's eyes were open and her lips moved, trying to form words. Amy chafed her hands, kneeling beside her on the floor. Then Grandma was there, sliding a pillow under Auntie's head and tossing the afghan from the couch over her still form.

"I'll call the doctor," she said to Amy. "Stay with her while I call the doctor."

Too soon she was back, kneeling beside Amy in her white flannel nightgown. "The phone's out," she said. "Matilda, can you hear me? Just lie quiet, we'll get help." She glanced up at the rain-battered windows. "Amy, I'll have to leave you here and go to the village myself."

But Amy was already on her feet, heading toward the stairs. "She needs you, Grandma. I wouldn't know what to do for her. Besides, I can run faster than you." In moments she had changed into pants and a sweater and grabbed her slicker and a flashlight from the pantry.

"I can't let you go into that storm, Amy."

"We haven't any choice, Grandma. You can't go, and Auntie needs a doctor. I'll take the shortcut to Betsy's house. Mr. Winters can help."

"But the brook's too high by now. You don't know the way."

"I'll find a way." Amy threw the latch on the heavy front door and yanked it open. The wind rushed in, thrusting Amy back against the lintel, tearing at the curtains and scattering ashes from the fireplace. Before Grandma could argue further,

Amy was out the door, running across the porch and into the wind and rain.

The momentum of her exit carried her as far as the front lawn, to the edge of the house. There she was stopped by the full force of the storm. The rain blew in sheets, nearly parallel to the ground, and Amy had to lean into the wind to keep from being blown backward. The beam of the flashlight glanced off the swirling rain, showing only the gray sodden grass directly in front of her. Head down, Amy pressed forward, toward the birch grove and the path down to Betsy's house.

"It hasn't been raining that long," she told herself. "The brook can't be too high to cross. If I can only find the path."

The wind tore back the hood of her slicker, forcing the rain down her neck and drenching her hair. Her pants legs clung dripping to her ankles, flapping heavily as she tried to run. Worst of all was the noise of the storm. The elm tree in the front yard hung clattering over the house, and the leaves and twigs leaped like live things from the ground to catch snapping on Amy's clothes. Over all was the rush of wind and pounding of rain. The normal murmur of the brook had been replaced by a steady roar that blended with that of the storm. Stumbling on longer grass, Amy realized that she had reached the meadow, but the familiar landmarks of trees and bushes, of the orchard behind the house, were invisible. She ran on, the beam of the flashlight bobbing ahead of her until suddenly the white trunks of the birches loomed up. Gasping for breath, she tripped into the grove and clung to one of the larger trees while she tried to get her bearings. Beneath her hand the tree trembled, thrumming to its very roots with the force of the wind that bent its branches nearly to the ground. Realizing she was below the path, Amy pressed on, pulling herself from one tree trunk to the next, moving diagonally toward the brook and the ford Betsy had showed her. The light was little use, serving only to point the way between the trees and to keep Amy from staggering into one of the low-hanging branches that swung toward her in the wind.

The flashes of lightning and the constant roll of thunder frightened her; stories of people hit by lightning and falling trees, or lost in flooded rivers, made her want to drop to the ground and huddle there until the storm passed. But each time she slowed down, the image of Auntie lying on the living room floor with Grandma beside her surfaced in her mind like some part of an endless nightmare. The fear that she would be too late to help the old woman drove her on.

"She can't die. She mustn't die." The words burst out in sobs as she broke through the thick grove of trees and stepped into water ankle deep. Amy stopped short and pointed the flashlight down. The shallow brook had overflowed its banks and rushed in a muddy current down the hillside. It pulled at her feet so that she stumbled with it along the bank where it beat higher and higher to the very roots of the birches. The stepping stones of the ford were gone, submerged in the steadily increasing volume of water. Catching hold of one of the trees, Amy stopped and swung the flashlight upstream. There was no sign of the flat white rock, only the wide rush of water tumbling down toward her. She was cut off from the village, from Ben and Betsy's house, unless she could reach the road before the stream covered the bridge.

The going was easier now, with the wind partially behind her as she left the grove and ran down the hill. Although the rain still fell heavily, the brunt of the storm was past; the lightning flashed distantly above the hills and the thunder was a far rumble beneath the sound of the driving rain. Once she stopped to look back to her right where the house and elm should have been on the crest of the hill, but could see only a faint shadow of white, no more, perhaps, than her memory of the worn, painted shingles. Ahead of her, she knew, was the church and the stone fence separating Seth's grave from the churchyard. As the meadow leveled out, Amy moved the flashlight in a wider arc, searching for the elm that marked his grave site. Strangely, there was nothing, not even a darker shape behind the rain to guide her. And then she was falling, tumbling and sliding down into muddy darkness, knowing too late what had happened.

She lay stunned in the pit of the huge elm's roots. The flashlight had been knocked from her hand when she pitched forward and still shone, miraculously, into the uprooted tree. Amy stared up at it, still dazed, remembering the crash of light and Auntie's cry as she had jumped from the rocking chair.

The elm was hit by lightning, she thought. The family tree. Even as she scrambled up, slipping on the mud, to retrieve the flashlight, Auntie's words fell into place. Not a paper family tree, not a history recorded in the family Bible, but a living tribute to Seth Howes. L . . . M is not a person, Auntie had said. Not a person, but the tree itself, the elm Lucy had planted to mark Seth's grave. Pulling herself up on the roots of the tree, Amy crawled through the branches that were splintered everywhere. In moments she had reached the fence, climbed over it, and was running through the churchyard toward the main road. Lucy's secret, kept for so many generations, would wait again on the living. Even the family legacy was not as important to Amy now as the life of the great-aunt she had so feared on her first day in the house on Constitution Hill. She ran hard along the road, her shoes squishing on the puddled macadam. At the bridge she saw the water only a foot beneath its highest point, the current heavier here where the narrowing steep banks of the stream closed in on the raging brook. Branches careened into the old wooden supports with echoing thuds, to be torn away by the torrent and thrown ahead to the other side. Amy could feel the wooden planks of the bridge shudder as she crossed, and then she was over it, on the other side, pounding again on the solid, deluged road. Somehow she went on, fighting against the wind, against the pain in her side, no longer conscious of the stiletto-cold drops that slashed at her face. The sharp points of the Winterses' white picket fence appeared beside her, then the opening of the gate, and then she was pounding, beating both fists on the solid, protected weight of Betsy's front door.

XVI

The Family Tree

A cold, clear light was shining through the windows the next morning, a winter light, stripped of the soft haze of autumn and polished by the violence of the storm. Amy opened her eyes slowly. She ached in every muscle; even her eyelids were stiff. She lay in her own spindle bed, the quilts pulled up around her chin, yet the room seemed unfamiliar. She looked from one object to the next, wondering what had changed, what was different. The house was unnaturally quiet, even for early morning; there was no rustle in the elm branches outside her window, all motion exhausted by the previous night. Amy's eyes rested finally on the acorn knob of the bedpost, and suddenly images of the night before cascaded through her mind: Mr. Winters pulling his trousers on over his pajamas while Mrs. Winters called the doctor on their static-ridden but still-functioning phone; Ben and Betsy standing quiet and white-faced beside her, awakened like their parents by her frantic pounding on the door. And then the long, wild drive back across the bridge, the water spewing up on each side of the car as they crossed and careened up the rain-rutted hill to the old house. There everything seemed to blur. The doctor, she remembered, disappeared into the living room while firm but gentle hands propelled her upstairs and into bed. Amy sat straight up, flinging the covers aside.

Auntie.

In one leap she was out of bed and across the room. She yanked open the door and stepped out into the dim, silent hallway. Her grandmother's room was empty, the bed neatly made or never slept in. The door to Auntie's room was closed. Were they still asleep? Or had they gone, taken Auntie away to a hospital while Amy slept, exhausted, through the remainder of the night? Or had her flight through the storm been in vain, had help been too late for Auntie?

Quietly she turned the knob and eased Auntie's door open. The curtains were drawn in the room, as they had been that first gray morning of her arrival, and for a moment she could see nothing. When her eyes adjusted, she saw Grandma seated at the foot of the bed in a rocker, dozing. On the far side of the bed in a straight-backed chair, the doctor sat with his chin on his chest, asleep. Amy looked at the bed. Auntie lay there, propped high on pillows, her fragile profile dimly white in the shuttered room. Afraid to move, to make any sound, Amy stood watching until she perceived the faint movement of Auntie's breathing. Her own breath came again in a rushing sigh of relief. She tiptoed to the side of the bed and stood there, looking down on the old woman, then reached out and laid her hand on Auntie's cold, folded ones.

"Please don't die," she whispered. "Please be all right. I need you." Tears slid down her cheeks, hot, frightened tears as startling to her as the truth of her feeling for this stern, determined old woman. The years between them had telescoped, the old life encompassing the young with understanding of dreams and hopes, the young supporting the old with new energy. Her fear of sightless age was gone, and Amy wanted nothing more than to share the present with Auntie as they had come to share the past. "Please, Auntie," she murmured, kneeling and leaning her head on the soft quilt, "please get better. I love you."

The thin, gnarled hand fluttered beneath her own, slid out, and brushed Amy's tangled braids. She looked up.

Auntie's eyes were open, and her pale lips moved soundlessly. "All right, child. No tears for me." She smiled, a mere creasing at the corners of her mouth that managed to brighten her whole face. "The book?"

"Yes, Auntie." Amy blinked rapidly, swiping at her eyes with one hand and clutching Auntie's hand with the other. "I understand now. I'll find it. You rest. I'll find it."

The old woman nodded and closed her eyes, still smiling the small, strange smile. Gently Amy placed her hands again on the quilt, brushed a kiss on the soft, thin cheek, and tiptoed out of the room.

It took her only a few minutes to dress in dungarees and a heavy flannel shirt. She carried her shoes downstairs, stepping carefully on the center of the stair risers to avoid any creaking, which would wake her grandmother and the doctor. After gulping a glass of juice, and leaving a note on the kitchen table, she slipped out the back door, sat on the tilted porch to put on her shoes, and ran around the house to the meadow.

Even after being in the storm, still feeling the effects of its pounding on her, Amy was not prepared for the scene before her. The remaining leaves had been stripped from the trees that lined Bridge Street, and large branches covered the yard and road. Vaguely she remembered the lurching of Mr. Winters's car as they approached the house, and she realized now that he had miraculously threaded his way through the tangle of debris the storm had torn down. The meadow itself was flattened, the brown grass bent and heavy with water. To her left the birch grove stood white and still, many of the trees broken off by wind and the weight of rain. Everywhere there were broken branches and twigs, and near the house, chunks of shingle. The valley was clearly visible through the stripped trees. Amy thought she could make out the white line of the Winterses' picket fence. Here on the crest of the hill the silence was less than total. There were the faint, early-morning bird sounds, and beneath them, the deep, unexpected roar of the swollen brook. From where she stood, Amy could not see the bridge, whether it had survived the rush of water from the hills. There was only the wide, muddy brook tumbling out of the birch grove, following the widened channel of the stream, and disappearing behind the church. Finally Amy looked down at the churchyard, to the place where Seth Howes's grave was marked by the towering elm. But the elm was gone, toppled by the storm, and lay with its heavy mass of branches facing south, its roots swung up to the light, leaving the massive pit into which Amy had fallen the night before. She started down the hill toward it.

Like the surviving elm in the yard of the farm, this tree had been a giant, its trunk too thick for Amy to put her arms around. And although she had seen it each morning when she looked out her window, it had never seemed as monumental as it did now, stretched on its side across the meadow. The entire view was different, somehow no longer balanced without the weight of the second elm, which had been part of the line from the farm to the church steeple.

Amy walked all around it, making a wide circle of the upper branches. Then she sat down on the trunk, patting it apologetically, and stared at the crown of roots.

It would help if I knew what to look for, she thought. It is the family tree, the L . . . M Lucy talked about. And if the key opens her book, then she must have put the book in the tree, in a hollow of the trunk, maybe, or in one of the branches.

She got up and inspected the trunk, feeling underneath where she could not see, then moved farther up to the large lower branches. But the tree was solid, and anything that had been placed in the now wide crotches of the branches was long gone, or swallowed up by the growth of the tree. She returned to the roots, considering their splintered yellow spikes, marveling that the storm had been powerful enough to bring the tree down. For almost two hundred years it had sheltered and cooled Seth's grave, from the time that Lucy had first dug the small hole and planted the sapling there for the man she loved.

What was it Betsy had said? If Lucy had buried the legacy with him, they could never find it. And if she had buried the unprotected book with the sapling, it would be long gone, absorbed into the soil. Which meant that she had buried the prayer book in something. Amy ran around the roots and looked down into the pit she had climbed out of the night before. The rain had washed away all traces of her footsteps, and a large, muddy puddle was cradled below the roots. On the far side was Seth's gravestone, mud splashed and tilted, but intact. Slowly Amy made her way around the edge of the hole, pulling back the long meadow grass, loosing the rocks that lay exposed in the dirt. She had come full circle before she saw it.

At the southern edge of the pit, imprisoned in the cracked and twisted roots that still clung to the dirt, was a brick-shaped object. Had she not been looking for it, she would have assumed that it was nothing more than a builder's brick that had found its way deep into the soil. Balancing herself on the edge of the depression, holding onto the tree trunk, Amy reached across and tried to pull the object free. It held, anchored in the dirt and roots. Amy stepped back, found a pointed branch, and slid into the hole. She dug and pried at the box, sinking deep into the mud, splattering herself with it and coating the knees of her dungarees as she leaned into the wall of dirt the tree had left. Finally the box came loose, and Amy pulled it from the safe haven where Lucy had put it so many years ago.

Shaking with the effort and excitement, mindless of the mud oozing around her ankles and through the heavy material of her pants, Amy leaned back against the roots and rubbed the dirt away from her find. It was a small casket of stone, marble perhaps, with a carved top, brought how many years ago, and by whom, to the new country as a gift to some unnamed ancestor. Amy looked carefully around the edges, not wanting to break it in an effort to open it, but it seemed to have no hinges, only the tight-fitting lid. Very gently she lifted it, pulling on the slight edge below the carving.

Inside was the black book, its cover mildewed and the gold clasp tarnished, but the book itself, intact.

For a moment Amy couldn't move, could only stand and stare at it. Tears pricked again at her eyes, blurring the outlines of the box.

"Auntie," she whispered. "I found it."

Clutching the box and cover to her chest, using the sharp stick for leverage, she clambered out of the hole and started running, mud caked, up the hill toward the farm. Tears continued to streak her face as she ran, and nearing the house, she began to shout.

"Auntie, Auntie, I found it!"

She careened up the front steps, slammed the door open and was halfway up the stairs before Grandma and the doctor appeared on the landing, shushing her. Behind her in the living room she had a glimpse of Mr. Winters, tousled from sleeping on the couch, staring at her from the doorway, his mouth open to speak.

"Amy, for the love of heaven, where have you been? You mustn't wake her. She has to rest."

But Amy charged past them, scattering dirt and mud, her feet leaving large, clotted tracks on the stairs.

"It will make her better, you'll see," she cried, and burst into Auntie's room, the doctor and Grandma fluttering behind her. "Auntie, I found it!"

She dropped to her knees beside the bed and placed the muddy casket in Auntie's hands. The old woman smiled and nodded, her eyes closed, as Amy pulled the top off the box and took out the prayer book. Auntie held it in one hand, and with the tips of her fingers felt the cover, the clasp, the stamp of the gold cross in the old leather. The doctor reached across Amy and took Auntie's wrist in his hand, feeling her pulse.

"Now, Miss Matilda," he said. "You can't go getting yourself all excited. You've got to rest until we can get you to the hospital for some tests."

Auntie's eyes flashed open and she glared at him a moment before shifting her gaze to Amy. "The key," she murmured, "get the key, child."

Amy stood up, aware at last of Grandma's insistent tugging at her sleeve, and allowed herself to be hurried out of the room.

"Have you no sense at all, Amy Enfield?" Grandma said when they were out in the hall. It was the first time Amy could remember hearing her grandmother really angry. "She is a sick woman, and you should know better than to get her excited now of all times, over things that are better left unknown."

"But they aren't better left unknown, Grandma. It matters to Auntie, and to me. She has something to live for now."

"Having something to live for doesn't keep people alive. If anyone knows that, I do. The doctor thinks she's had a stroke, or at least collapsed from sheer exhaustion. I let her do too much for that party, and I'm not going to have you making her worse with this legacy business. Now, you get yourself cleaned up, and then you can get the mud off the stairs and hallway."

"You don't understand, Grandma." Amy spoke quietly, the need to open the book with Auntie more important than her grandmother's anger with her. "We have to see what's in that book. Auntie's waited her whole life to find it. If you make her wait any longer, it may be too late."

"Don't argue with me, young lady. Since when do you know better than the doctor?"

"Perhaps she does," the doctor said, closing the door behind him and looking curiously at Amy. "I can't determine the damage to her heart or anything else without the equipment I don't have here. She's a stubborn woman, Louise, and if she doesn't have some time with this young lady of yours, she'll do more damage . . . out of spite, I think." He turned and smiled at Amy. "Fifteen minutes, Amy, and that's all. It's true that happiness can heal, but the body needs rest and quiet to help the healing along. Hurry up, now, and do what she wants."

Amy hugged him, leaving a stain of mud on his rumpled white shirt, then grabbed Grandma's hands and squeezed them in both of her own. "It's all right, really. I'm sorry I made you angry, but it's important, honest."

She pulled away then and ran down the hall to her own room, snatched the key from its hiding place in the acorn knob, and raced back to Auntie. Her fingers trembling, she placed the gold key in the lock and gently turned it. The clasp fell open, the leather cracking as the hinge opened. She handed it to Auntie.

"You open it. You've waited so long."

"No, child. It is yours."

Glancing at Auntie's pale, tense face, Amy did not argue. She turned back the cover of the prayer book. In the flyleaf was written "Lucy Coburn," scratched in an ornate, immature script. Beside it, obviously added years later, was written "Howes."

" 'Lucy Coburn Howes,' " Amy read softly, touching the lines with her finger. "Auntie, he was her husband."

The old woman nodded.

"You knew?" Questions tangled around all Amy knew or thought she had known of her ancestor, webbing through the efforts Lucy had made to reach them. But Amy pushed the thoughts aside and turned to the first page of the book. Inside was a space for listing marriages, births, and deaths. In the same hand was recorded the following:

Lucy Coburn married Seth Howes, Albany, 1782.

Seth Howes died, 1783.

Lucy Coburn Howes married Charles Griffin, 1783.

Charles Howes Griffin born, 1783.

Below it, dated October 3, 1783, was the beginning of a lengthy entry, written in the same hand, which filled the blank first pages of the prayer book and extended onto the ones in the back of the book. Amy stared at it, and for a moment the words seemed to blur, as though she heard rather than read them. Images of Lucy in her room, in the attic, at the white rock among the birches, blotted out the whispery writing. Lucy's presence filled the room, not as she had appeared to Auntie or Amy, but with the powerful sense of the past about to be revealed. Holding the spidery words to the light, Amy began to read.

XVII

The Legacy

" 'By the time you read these words, my child, you will already know in part the legacy I have left you. It is a heritage of pain, born of hate which tore this new country from England, hate over which neither your father nor I had control. Our world is gone, destroyed in the upheaval of a war I barely understand, which has taken from me brothers, husband, father. I am hiding now the truth of your past, to protect you from the bitterness of those who would take vengeance even on the innocence of the unborn. And I bow to my father's will even though I reject his right to impose it, because of the fate his blindness has inflicted upon us all. Years from now, when hate and ill will have died, you will come upon this book. Then can your birthright be claimed, its symbol returned to its rightful place. I have left a message in the family Bible to guide you.' "

"But there was nothing in the Bible, Auntie, even in your time." Amy looked up from the book, remembering the brittle, yellowed pages of the family Bible, the faded brown writing that listed the family names, births, and deaths. No record of Lucy's was left there.

"Could she have changed her mind?"

Auntie shook her head. "Philo Coburn," she whispered. "He was as blind as I have been, trying to change the future by denying the past. Go on, child, read."

Amy returned to the book. " 'Seth Howes is dead. My husband is dead. Your father is dead, by the hand of my own father. Once trusted friend and priest, a welcome guest in our house, Seth Howes became my father's enemy, his loyalty to the Crown and the king's church anathema to Philo Coburn's patriotism. We wed in secret, without his consent, through the aid of a trusted friend in Albany. It was a brief union. I returned to my father's house to seek his blessing. Confronted with the fact of our marriage, my father locked me away, determined to annul what he had been unable to prevent. I could get no message to Seth; my father would listen to no plea to let me go with my husband to England. Seth waited in vain, defending beyond reason or hope the church he served. In the end the British troops were driven from the town. The patriots billeted their men in the churchyard, used our blessed communion table for their captain's meals, and drove Seth out at risk to his life.

" 'Only then did he come for me, trusting in my faith if not my love, come to retrieve from me the Queen Anne silver he had entrusted to me for safekeeping. Even as I strove to escape my father's house, to join Seth no matter what the cost, he came to me, to his death. I saw him cross the meadow, saw him struck down by Philo Coburn's shot. A renegade, my father thought him. He died there in the deep meadow grass, believing me to be both faithless and untrue.

" 'The townspeople would do him no honor. Memory of his kindness was lost in the passion for freedom from the crown. They allowed no loyalist to be buried in the churchyard; Seth was laid in a criminal's grave outside the church, marked only by my hand and this sapling which I plant today.

" 'He died thinking that I had betrayed him, forsaken him to remain in the house of my birth. He died knowing nothing of you, my child. From that bitter judgment I have no recourse. But I have sworn to keep his legacy from those who would desecrate it as they have dishonored his memory. Only when he receives his rightful burial beside his church shall the silver be returned to its altar.

" 'I wed a man whose child you appear to be. He is a good man, Charles Griffin. I pray that he and his family will accept us both.' "

"But they didn't, did they, Auntie? Accept her. Do you think they guessed he wasn't Charles Griffin's son?"

Auntie turned one hand palm up, questioning also. She spoke in a dry, thin whisper. "Perhaps his sons feared the loss of their inheritance. Perhaps they knew. But they sent her back to her father when Charles Griffin died. There was no love lost between them and Lucy."

"We'll never know now." Amy sighed and read the next line.

" 'All reason, all compassion have fled my life. I shall live a lie in order to uphold the truth; I shall dishonor one husband to protect another; I shall bury this legacy to insure its inheritance. My only peace shall be in death, my only honor when your name shall be acknowledged.' "

"But Auntie," Amy interrupted herself. "Couldn't she see?"

The old woman opened her eyes.

"Couldn't she see that her anger would only make things worse? The church survived, and the war...." Amy paused. "The war changed everything. There would have been no United States."

"History, our history was her present. She knew only the losses—husband, family, future. Try to understand. She could not know what this country was to be, what she had bought with those losses."

One paragraph remained. Amy touched the words as though the physical contact could help her to understand Lucy's grief. All the sadness, all the pain the old house had witnessed, was there, there beneath her fingertips. She took a deep breath and read on.

" 'I could not carry the silver with me to my new home, lest it be found out and my sworn trust revealed. I have hidden it here in this house, among the common items of our household, seen but unrecognized beneath the tarnish which will be its own shield. Our family's past is intertwined now with Seth's own, as the vines of our grapes are grown together. You are the child of that union, as the wine is the fruit of the grape. Seek out the cup and paten there, and return them to your father's church.' "

There was nothing else. Amy turned the pages front and back, but Lucy had written no more.

"Auntie, that's all. What does she mean?"

"The wine, child, the wine. Wine for the church was made here."

"But so long ago. How could she expect him to understand her riddles? How can I?"

"Think as she did, Amy," Auntie said, reaching for the girl's hand. "Think as she did."

"You called me Amy." Startled at hearing her name from the old woman's lips, Amy looked up quickly. She had become accustomed to Auntie's addressing her only as "child," to being that child who was a means to the past, a second chance for Auntie to reach out to Lucy Griffin. Auntie's hand tightened on her own, the bond between them now complete. No longer strangers, they were both part of the line that stretched back over the decades to the spidery handwriting in Lucy's prayer book, a line that twisted and wound other families, other histories, other deaths, with their own, in a skein as tangled as the vines that once grew on their land.

"It's time, Amy." Grandma touched her on the shoulder. "Aunt Matilda must rest now."

"Yes, ma'am." Slowly Amy stood up, but Auntie held her back.

"Think, Amy," she whispered again. "Think and remember. You are the child of her past."

Still carrying the book, Amy returned to her room, to Lucy's room, where she had dreamed her dreams of Seth Howes and been locked away from him at Philo Coburn's will. Amy went to the window and looked out over the storm-flattened meadow. Even in the clear, washed daylight she could see again the events of her dream, imagine Seth running out of the birch grove and across the long grass to his death. That shot had shattered peace in the old house for over a century and a half; Amy could restore it now by answering Lucy's shadowy plea from the past. She closed her eyes, trying to empty her mind of everything but her knowledge of her ancestor.

"Think as she did," she told herself, as pictures and words tumbled out in her mind. And suddenly, she knew where to find the silver. The image was there, as clear as the sharp scent of Grandma's chrysanthemums, as bright as the jars of preserves on the shelves of the root cellar. Quietly she ran down the stairs, pausing in the doorway of the living room. Lucy's portrait was framed in a full square of sunlight. Amy was struck, as she had been on first sight of the painting, by the contradiction of the smiling eyes in the serious face. It was a young and happy face, and the hands folded over the prayer book in her lap were young, still unmarked by the hard farm work that was in store for her. The shadow of that future touched the painting; Amy saw Lucy's face as she had appeared in the attic, the mischievous beauty altered and saddened. For an instant the two faces blended, past and present melded, and Amy felt the chill of her own unknown years to come.

"It's all right, Lucy," she whispered into the still, sunlit room. "I'll bring it to you."

She turned then and went through the dining room to the kitchen and outside to the root cellar. The handle of the slanted door was cold to the touch, still shadowed by the bulk of the old house. Amy pulled up on the handle and swung the door back on its hinges, smelling the cool, damp, earthy smell of the room below. The stone steps were slippery with moisture from the night's rain, as though they had absorbed a portion of the deluge. Carefully Amy felt her way down the steps, reaching out into the darkness for the cord of the light switch. The cellar was just as Grandma had left it, the neat if dusty lines of preserves along the shelves, the wine press on the table, the old wooden cask lid leaning against the wall. She looked at it, noticing now not only the quality of the carving in the old wood, but the intertwining of the vines, the overlapping of individual grape leaves. Kneeling down, she rolled the lid aside and wriggled into the back of the cellar to the corner where Grandma and her brother Johnny had played while Uncle Plyn sampled his wine. There, where Grandma had placed them after showing them to Amy, were the blackened cup and plate.

Gently Amy picked them up, feeling the weight of the tarnished silver, wondering that she had touched them before and not recognized their value. Almost reluctantly she carried the chalice and paten out of the root cellar into the sunlight. After so many years in darkness, they should be received with ceremony, she thought, with singing and trumpets. And Lucy and Seth should be celebrated, their marriage honored. Stepping onto the damp grass, Amy paused to look over to the storm-broken, leafless birch grove, where the brook rushed now over the white rock on which her ancestors had met. She waited, cradling the silver in her arms, anticipating a triumphal surge of excitement. The legacy was found; Lucy's promise would be kept, her trust fulfilled, Seth's faith in her restored. But after all Amy's searching, after all her impatience with the mysteries of her heritage, all her eagerness to resolve the past, this moment of discovery was a hushed victory, cloaked in memory. It settled around Amy, a still, serene awareness of the completion of a mission. Its resolution freed Lucy and Seth, released Auntie from the quest for which she had clung to life, and gave Amy a glimpse of the precariousness of her own future. In that instant her own memories were one with Lucy's and Auntie's, their pasts existing as her present, her present spun away in an unknown future. And then the moment was gone, the hushed internal silence broken. Clutching the silver in sudden fear that she would drop it, Amy ran back to the house and into the kitchen.

As Amy came in the back door, she heard a tapping at the front. Still holding the silver in her arms, she ran to the vestibule and pulled open the door. Ben and Betsy stood on the porch with their mother, who was carrying a picnic basket and a kerosene lamp.

"We never even asked if you had lights last night," Mrs. Winters said, bustling past Amy. "Where is your grandmother? And how is Miss Matilda? The doctor's still here, I take it."

"Grandma's upstairs," Amy answered as Mrs. Winters paused for breath. "She and the doctor are still with Auntie. He wants to take her to the hospital if we can get through."

"The bridge is damaged, but passable. I've got the ambulance outside." With that, she started up the stairs, leaving her basket and lamp in the hallway.

"Is she going to be all right?" Betsy asked. Her brown eyes were round with worry. "You really scared us last night."

Ben nodded. "That was some hike you took. I don't know how you made it."

"I had to," Amy said. "But everything's going to be all right. Auntie's got to get better now. Look." She held out the cup and plate.

They stared at the blackened objects Amy held, frowning. Then Betsy's eyes widened even further. "You found it?" she gasped.

"That's the silver?" Ben shook his head. "It can't be."

"But it is!" Amy started to laugh then, bubbles of excitement building in her, filling out her chest and tightening in her throat. "Auntie figured it out, but if it hadn't been for the storm, I'd never have found the book. It needs to be polished, Ben, and blessed before the church can use it again, but it is the silver."

"You're giving it back?"

"Of course." But Amy stopped to think. Lucy had sworn to return the silver when Seth was returned to his church. Otherwise her promise would not be kept. "Of course we'll give it back, but not until the rector agrees to move Seth Howes's grave to its proper place beside Lucy. Come on. Let's see if they'll let us show Auntie."

They bounded up the stairs two at a time. Auntie's door was open, and Mrs. Winters and Grandma stood just inside the room talking in low voices. The doctor stood beside the bed, giving Mr. Winters instructions for the ambulance attendants. The three darted into the room. Amy touched the doctor's sleeve.

"Please, Dr. James, before she goes, I must show Auntie something." Without waiting for his permission, Amy slipped behind him and placed the chalice and paten in Auntie's lap.

"It was there, Auntie, in the root cellar. The legacy is found."

XVIII

In Pacem Requiescant

It was early spring, with crocuses blooming in the sunny corners of the meadow, springing out of the melting beds of snow. Bridge Street was muddy with the spring thaw, and along the roadbed the tree buds swelled. Fuzzy pussy willow had burst out beside the brook, and the willow trees in the valley were a hazy gold. On the south side of the church, where the sun had warmed the earth and the stone wall retained the heat through the lengthening days, daffodils were sprouting, their heavy blossoms drooping yellow. On the far side, in the churchyard, was a newly fenced-off and seeded plot. Amy stood in front of it, looking down at the white, carved marker.

"They got it right this time, Auntie," she said, turning to the woman who sat in the wheelchair beside her. " 'Lucy Coburn Howes Griffin,' it says. 'Howes her name in the sight of God.' And then it gives her dates. And under her name is Seth's, with his dates."

"And her son, Charles Howes?"

"Right there beside them. Can't you see it at all? Maybe we should come back when the sun is brighter."

"No sun will ever be brighter for me than this day's, not

until I see it in the hereafter. And there's space here for me?"

"The doctor says you won't have to worry about that for a long time. But, yes, there is. For all of us, I guess. I wish you could see it."

"You're my eyes, Amy, and served me better than my own." She looked down, feeling in the pocket of her dress for a handkerchief. "I'll miss you."

Amy's throat tightened. Blinking hard, she looked away to where her parents and grandmother stood in front of the church talking to the rector. "And I'll miss you. I wish in a way that I didn't have to go. But we'll be back this summer."

Auntie cleared her throat. "The service was well done, I thought."

"And the silver, Auntie, could you see the silver? It shines so!"

"I held it, Amy, and that was enough." She turned again toward the graves. "It's finished now for them, their promises kept. I wonder if they know."

"But they must know." Amy's gaze swung up the hill to the old house, to the window of her room. The white curtains moved in the spring breeze, and Amy thought of her suitcases packed and ready to go, set neatly at the foot of the spindle bed. "Auntie, there's something else I have to do. Do you want to wait here, or shall I take you over to Grandma?"

"I'll wait." She touched Amy's arm and looked up. "You will tell me what you see?"

"I'll tell you. I'll be right back."

She ran around the plot to the back of the churchyard, climbed over the fence and into the meadow. In a moment she had found the path to the birch grove, and followed it up the hill. The birches, too, were coming back, sprouting new branches from the breaks of the Halloween storm. Amy slowed down as she entered the grove and moved quietly toward the brook. Grass was growing now where the water had overrun its banks, and although the brook was high, the flat, white rock gleamed in the sunlight. Amy stood still among the birches, watching, listening to the voice of the water as it ran its course downhill. She concentrated on the shimmering white trunks of the birches, squinting against the sparkle of the rushing brook, remembering Seth and Lucy, willing them to return once more.

"Just to say good-by," she whispered, her voice blending with the rustle of the birch leaves. But there was only the memory to bring the past beyond the curtain of the present. Amy's fingernails dug half-moon indentations into her palms with the effort to recall her ancestors. Suddenly she relaxed and opened her eyes. They were gone, and it was right that they did not return. Their lives resolved at last, their promises kept, they could be one in the peace they each had sought. Amy smiled. Her past, too, had meshed with theirs, with Auntie's, with her family's, and now the future fluttered greenly ahead. "Good-by," she whispered again.

"Aunt Matilda said I'd find you here."

Amy jumped at the sound of the low voice behind her and spun around. "Ben! You startled me."

"Sorry. I didn't want you to leave without saying good-by."

"I know." Amy smiled again. "That's what I was doing."

Ben glanced at the rock, then back to Amy. "Did you see them?"

"No. And I shouldn't have expected to. Auntie was right."

"About how we'd change?"

"About how everything changes. If they were still here, we would have failed."

Ben nodded, and for a moment they stood looking at the stream together in silence. Then Ben reached in his pocket.

"Betsy and I thought, that is, I thought, that you ought to

have something to remember this year by. So you don't forget us," he added in a rush. Reaching out, he grabbed her hand and placed in the palm a small box. "Here. For you."

"Should I open it?"

"How else will you know what's in it?" Ben frowned at her and jammed both hands back in his pockets. Amy untied the string and lifted the lid of the box. Inside was a silver medal of St. George. She lifted it out, its silver spinning lights across the birch grove.

"There's something on the back," Ben mumbled. Clearing his throat, he looked away from Amy to the flashes of light.

Amy turned the medal over and read the inscription: "To Amy Enfield, friend, from Ben and Betsy Winters."

She stood there with the silver disc on her palm, the inscription blurring through sudden, unexpected tears.

"I guess it was a pretty dumb thing to do," Ben growled, glancing at her and turning away.

"No, Ben, wait." She reached out to him. "It's just that it's beautiful. But even without it, I'd never forget you, or Betsy."

"It isn't anything much." Slowly Ben turned back to her. Lifting the medal on its chain from the box, he hung it gently around her neck. "Besides, you'll be back this summer."

"I'll be back this summer." Amy smiled up at him. "Thank you, friend."

Ben grinned. "Come on. We'd better get back before your parents send out a search party."

Taking her hand, he turned and started down the path. Amy glanced once more to the rock, sure now that she would see no more of Lucy and Seth. Behind her as she left the grove, the brook murmured in its treble and baritone voices of the past.